MISADVENTURES

AT

CITY HALL

MISADVENTURES

AT

CITY HALL

BY
VICTORIA BLUE

WATERHOUSE PRESS

Copyright © 2019 Waterhouse Press, LLC
Cover Design by Waterhouse Press.
Cover images: Shutterstock

ISBN: 978-1-64263-142-5

For David —
I can't remember an adventure without you!

CHAPTER ONE

The first day back to the office after a major upheaval is a lot like the first day of freshman year in high school. Stick close to your friends and keep your head down in the hallway.

Most importantly, wear your best outfit because you never know whom you might sit next to in biology.

"Skye, have you read this?" said Tara, my stall mate, as we liked to call each other. She came around the corner of our semiprivate office, holding a memo in her hand like it was a viper rather than a piece of paper.

"Who's it from?" I hadn't checked my mailbox this morning, so I hadn't seen the memo, and I was logging in to my computer when she came around the corner, so I hadn't read my email either.

"It's from Bailey Hardin. She's resigning," Tara said, staring at the paper in disbelief.

I shrugged while waiting for Tara to glance up. "Well, no one expected her to stay on, did they? I mean, think about it. She came from finance, she has no experience, and the only reason Mayor Roberts appointed her city manager when her husband passed was because he thought she was in on all his crooked bullshit. She played along so she could fry everyone— including the mayor."

The fact that I still had to explain the situation to my coworkers was the reason I would rise above them. They all heard and saw the exact same press conference I did yesterday. Hell, we had front-row seats for the three-ring circus. The fallout should not have come as a surprise.

Of course, what my coworkers hadn't been privy to happened after the press conference, when all the arrests had been made. When the dust settled and everyone went home, I went to Bailey Hardin's office to hand in my resignation, because as far as I could tell, my career at the Los Angeles City Manager's Office was over.

Yes, me, the go-getter. I had my eye on the prize—focused and determined. I was so driven, I'd even put up with William Hardin, the former city manager of Los Angeles, a true asshole of a boss. My career plan was set. I would work my butt off for Hardin, get noticed by the people who mattered in city hall, and when the election cycle turned, I would score an appointment higher in the ranks. Eventually I'd run for an elected position and continue my way up to the state legislature.

One day, if I kept my nose clean and my ducks in a row, I'd have a Georgetown address.

It was a great plan. Flawless.

Until that bastard Hardin up and died with a tartelette honey riding his dick in a seedy motel somewhere in West Hollywood. The two had a few too many hits of some concoction of MDMA, and old Willy's heart threw in the towel.

That should have been good news—for my career, obviously, not for him. I thought I might be the obvious choice to fill Hardin's shoes. Except his wife, Bailey, swooped in—from the finance department, of all places—and took the position, accepting the appointment from the former mayor.

I could have coped with that. But Bailey took the position so she could clean house, from top to bottom. This place was as dirty as the city dump. After she'd done her due diligence, she'd held a press conference, and *voila!* Half of city hall was led out in handcuffs.

Which was great for Los Angeles, don't get me wrong, but now that Bailey was resigning, my position as assistant to the city manager was in jeopardy. New boss, new team.

"Can you field my calls for a few minutes?" I asked my coworker. "On second thought, I'll put my phone on *do not disturb.*" I figured that was safer rather than letting her speak to anyone who called me.

Control freak? Maybe.

Walking down the hall, I passed a few offices that were now empty. Just two days ago, people sat at these desks, busy behind computers, on telephones, and shuffling papers. Amazing what a little knowledge and a lot of balls can do to an organization.

I knocked softly on Bailey's door and waited for her to call for me to come in. When I opened her door, I was surprised to find a few banker boxes on the desk, already packed and ready to go.

"Grass doesn't grow under your feet, does it?" I teased.

"Well, I didn't really have too much in here. I spent more time working in my office over in finance before William passed." She looked thoughtful. "God, that still seems weird to say at times. Then there are the days it seems like he's been gone for years. Is that bad?" She looked at me with a troubled expression, and honestly, I had no idea how to respond.

"I...uh...well, I don't really have much to draw from, you know? I mean, my father passed when I was a little girl, but I never knew him anyway. But other than that..." I probably made her feel worse with my answer.

"Oh, I'm sorry. About your dad, I mean," Bailey replied.

"No, don't be. Absolute stranger." I waved my hand dismissively. "Never met him. Not once."

Well, that was a conversation killer if I'd ever dealt one. She awkwardly shuffled the few papers left on her desk before I put her out of her misery and spoke again.

"So, the reason I stopped in... I saw your interoffice memo this morning—"

"Right, I wanted to talk to you about that too."

"Really? What about it? Looks like your decision is pretty final." I looked around the office pointedly. "I mean, you announced it to the staff." What input of mine could she have needed?

"No, I'm definitely not cut out for the city manager spot. Everyone knows that. I think you've had a few colorful ways of expressing the thought yourself." She gave me a playful wink while reminding me of my awful recent behavior.

Bailey had not only affected my professional life, but she'd also crossed into my private world too. She'd hooked up with my best friend and roommate, Oliver. At first I wasn't very supportive, but now they are head over heels in love, Oliver has moved in with her, and I'm officially on my own.

"I've apologized for that. To you and Oliver. I'm not sure

what else I can do, Bailey." I stood my ground, owning the fact that apologies were not my forte.

She put her hand up to stop my mea culpa. "That's not what I meant. I was simply teasing you. I'm not very good at the whole 'playful' thing. Oliver's trying his best to help me 'lighten up,' as he puts it."

A genuine smile warmed her face. She truly loved Oliver, and it did good things to my heart to see those emotions run across her face.

"I'm very happy for the two of you," I told her, hoping she could sense my sincerity. Many people in our line of work had a stellar bullshitting ability, but I meant what I said.

When Oliver and Bailey first started dating, I was very jealous. I had never had to share him with anyone else. Not in a lover sort of way, of course—it was never that way between us—but in a human companion sort of way. I was spoiled with Oliver always being there for me, literally and figuratively. Once he started seeing Bailey, his attention shifted fully, and it was hard for me to adjust.

My professional life was in upheaval at the same time, turning me into a self-contained category five hurricane. For a month or so, every time Hurricane Skye touched down, Oliver was directly in my path. He caught the brunt of every bad mood, insecure freak-out, and anxiety-driven breakdown.

In the beginning, he weathered the storm like a true champion. He tried to batten down the hatches and ride it out like a trooper. Eventually he started digging in and standing his ground, though, and looking back, I couldn't say I blamed him. I took a lot of work-related stress out on him when I would get home, and he hadn't deserved that. When the proverbial shit finally hit the fan, he headed for higher ground and moved in with Bailey. When the storm waters receded, I'd owed them both a huge apology for my behavior, and luckily, they both had gracious, forgiving hearts and still called me their friend.

Bailey cleared her throat, bringing me back to our conversation. "I wanted to talk to you about your professional plans. I mean from this point forward. What are you thinking?"

"That's a good question. Before this morning, I thought I would ride it out as your assistant until the election. At least that would give me a little more time to come up with a modified plan."

"What was your original plan, then?" she went on relentlessly. "Say, before William died?"

"Originally, I hoped I would take his job." I grinned. "Seriously, I thought I would show my worth around here, the next cycle would pass, and whoever took the mayoral race would appoint me to manager." I shrugged because to me, it seemed like the next logical step.

"Okay, that makes perfect sense." She nodded. "What was on the master plan after city manager?"

"Wait. What? You know about my master plan? Who told you about that?" My voice rose in panic. "Oliver doesn't even know about that." Should I be embarrassed about my neurotic planning habits?

"Skye." She touched my forearm to center me. "Every smart woman has a master plan. Or at least I thought they did. I always have. I still do. Although now I know better, and I use a pencil. Because life changes. Inevitably, things change that you can't control. The older you get and the more people you have in your circle, the more your plan changes." Now she was the one grinning. "And I'm a neat freak. All the crossing out, white out, and smudges were driving me crazy, so I started using a pencil. I can breathe again when I look at my planner."

I narrowed my eyes with a playful grin on my lips. "We may have been separated at birth."

"That would explain a lot from Oliver's standpoint."

"Right?" I nodded, thinking seriously about the point she just made.

"Back to the conversation, though." Bailey had a great way of keeping a conversation on point. "Where do you see yourself after city manager?"

"Mayor," I said instantly. "Well, at least a city council seat."

"Why?" She fired her question so fast, I felt like I was in a job interview. A tough one at that.

"Because they're elected offices, and it's the first level. I think it would be the best spot to get my feet wet running a campaign and gauging my appeal with the voters." I nodded, satisfied with my response.

"I'm really impressed, Skye. You've done your homework." She leaned on the edge of her empty desk.

"Thanks...I guess. No offense, but how does my career path concern or, rather, interest you?"

"Well, I'm invested," she said. "I want more than to see you land on your feet after what's happened here. I want to see you land and take off running, you know? I want to see you succeed. I was very driven by your age. I see a lot of myself in you." She smiled in a motherly way, even though she wasn't even ten years older than me.

"Thank you, Bailey. I'll take all of those words as compliments." I hesitated and then decided I had to ask the question. "I have to still press this issue, though. With you resigning, where does that leave me? Who will take your place? The entire city government is in shambles. How can we possibly have an election in a week when half of the candidates have withdrawn from the race?" There were a lot of unanswered questions around city hall.

"Well, don't quote me on this," she said as she walked past me and closed her door completely, ensuring no one could overhear her. "It's my understanding there has been a petition sent to Sacramento to postpone the election." She turned back to me to gauge my reaction.

"Really? That would be the first time in the city's history, I think," I said with astonishment.

"Possibly. I'm not certain. Regardless, it would be significant. But it would also give you time to organize a campaign if you were interested in doing so." She stared at me expectantly.

"Wait. What are you saying? You think I should run for the mayor of Los Angeles?" Surprise made my voice climb an octave.

"Whoa there, sister. Let's not get ahead of ourselves." She chuckled and sat against her desk again. "I think a spot on the city council is very likely going to be vacated. I've heard serious talk from a few of the current seat holders about running for mayor. Of course, they have the experience needed and the trust of the voters. You, my dear, would make perfect sense to fill a spot left behind on the city council."

While I felt like a total ass for aiming so high right out of the gate and being shot down the way I'd been, I was intrigued by the idea of running for city council. Plus, it basically skipped an entire step on my master plan, making up for the lag created by William's death.

"This is a very interesting idea," I said. And then I thought of all the reasons it wouldn't work. "There's so little time, though. I mean, I'm not shying away from a good challenge, but there's not even time for an exploratory committee or any of the usual pre-campaign steps."

"You're not wrong," she said, arms crossed over her chest.

"I don't know. Maybe this isn't the right time for my first campaign, you know, on such an abbreviated schedule?" Doubt already niggled at my gut.

"Maybe not. Only you can decide that."

"Why are you being so vague?" I asked her.

"I'm not being vague."

"You totally are."

She uncrossed her arms and sighed. "These aren't questions for me to answer, Skye. If you don't have the conviction to answer a few simple questions about your own campaign, you're right, you probably aren't ready to run for public office." She stood from where she had been perched on the edge of her desk, seeming to have lost patience with me.

"I didn't say I wasn't ready," I protested, sounding like a child.

"Didn't you?"

"No, I didn't." I tried to sound more convincing.

"Then stop acting like it."

She went to her door and opened it. She said nothing at all and just stood there.

"Are you kicking me out?" I looked at her, confused.

"Am I?" she asked.

"Oh, my God. Are you always this infuriating?" I had a serious impulse to flick her nose.

"Do you always answer your own questions with another question?" She tilted her head marginally to the side.

"This is why Oliver always loses arguments," I finally said, realizing I did the exact same thing to him.

"I know. Isn't it awesome?" Her grin was wider than I had seen on her face before.

We high-fived each other as I passed by on the way out the door.

"So, are you going to file the papers?" she asked my retreating back.

I paused and turned. Now that I was in the hall, I didn't want to broadcast my intentions to the rest of the office. "I need to think about it," I said quietly. "It's a serious step. I need to check my financial picture above all else."

"Don't wait too long. The clock is ticking. Literally," Bailey replied.

"I know. Is this something you want to be involved in? Long-term, I mean?" Now it was her turn to be in the hot seat.

"Present me with an offer I can't turn down," she said and shrugged. "We'll talk about it. As of this afternoon, I'm unemployed. I don't think the finance department wants me back."

"I'll be in touch," I called over my shoulder as I walked down the hall toward my office. Or, as we called it, the veal-fattening pen.

Tara pounced the minute I returned. "You were gone a long time. What's going on? Did you get some dirt? Did she get fired?"

"Did who get fired?" I played dumb, as if I hadn't just been in Bailey's office the whole time.

"Oh." She looked crestfallen. "I thought you went to talk to Ms. Hardin."

"Nah, I was in the can. My stomach can't handle all this drama. Plus, I drank too much last night, and now I'm paying for it. You know how the day after tequila feels." I held my stomach for maximum effect.

"Oh, God!" She put her hand up to stop me. "Don't even mention tequila. After the last office happy hour, I can't even hear the T-word without turning green."

I decided to email my closest girlfriend, Laura. We were roommates in college and still got together when our schedules allowed. Laura was a smart woman and the perfect sounding board for so many things in my life because she had nothing to do with politics.

She sent an answering message right away, and we agreed to have drinks after work. Luckily the tequila story I'd told Tara was just that—a story—so the idea of meeting at a watering hole sounded like just what the doctor ordered. The workday couldn't end soon enough.

CHAPTER TWO

"Thanks for meeting me on such short notice," I said to my friend around a bite of sinful Buffalo wing. The ice-cold beer delivered by the waitress was going to wash down the spicy hot wing sauce perfectly.

"And miss a gourmet dinner like this? No way!" Laura grinned as she shoved a tortilla chip full of some of the best guacamole in Los Angeles into her mouth. It was one of the main reasons we repeatedly visited Itza's. That and the three-dollar drafts until eight on Thursdays. And what do you know? It was Thursday. Things were looking up already.

"Well? Tell me what's going on. I mean, I love the ambiance in this classy joint as much as the next girl, but I can feel the tension in the air around you from where I'm sitting. So spill your guts while I fill mine with this green goopy heaven." She shoveled another chip into her mouth and scooted her bar stool closer to mine at the bistro table we'd claimed near the corner of the room.

"You know, I always think I have this fabulous poker face, and then you or Oliver burst my bubble and call me on my shit. Can't you just let me have a moment?"

She shrugged, her mouth full again.

"Not even one?" I laughed at the pace at which she was

chowing down. "Are you fucking pregnant or something? You're eating like you haven't had food in weeks."

"Actually, funny you should mention that."

"Wait. Whaaa? But—wait. Who? No. Are you sure?" I was rambling like an idiot. Laura was unattached and very career-driven. How on earth could she have let something like this happen?

"Are you sure you're a politician in training? I've watched these people on TV, Skye. You're going to have to get better at the whole 'talking' thing." She made air quotes while grinning. She was pretty upbeat for a woman in crisis.

"What are you going to do? I mean, are you one hundred percent sure you're pregnant? It's not a false positive?" I lowered my voice to a whisper in case there was anyone we knew in the bar. A lot of people we both knew came to Itza's regularly.

"I saw a doctor this morning. I'm nine weeks, so it's very early. But absolutely positive. I saw the little tiny heartbeat. It was incredible, actually." The wistful look on her face confused me more than anything she said.

"Laura. What the hell is going on here?" I waited until she looked directly at me and stopped scarfing down guacamole like her life—and apparently the life of another—depended on it.

"I've known you for a really long time. And for as long as I've known you, you've never once talked about wanting a child. Now you randomly toss out the fact that you're preggers like you're telling me you got a cute skirt on sale at Neiman's." I waved my hand in the air dismissively. "Then you look all dreamy when answering the follow-ups." I bugged my eyes out at her. "What the hell is going on with you?"

She smiled slyly, and that was when I noticed she hadn't ordered a beer. She had a Sprite sitting in front of her and was toying with the straw instead of answering my questions. Finally I covered her hand with mine, and she looked up and met my expectant stare.

"Laura, tell me what's going on," I implored.

"I decided to be a surrogate for my sister." Her pride radiated outward, enough to light the dim bar.

"Oh, my God. Why didn't you tell me?" I stumbled off my stool and into her arms, hugging her with my entire body. When I pulled back from the embrace, I looked at my friend. "How amazing is this? Seriously, that is the most beautiful, giving, selfless thing one woman could do for another woman. Oh, my God, I seriously think I'm going to cry." I held up my index finger dramatically. "Wait...no. I was close, though. It almost happened. Regardless, so proud of you."

Laura covered her face with both hands for a few seconds, taking the time to pull herself together emotionally, I assumed. Neither one of us were fans of expressing our feelings.

"I'm sorry to Bogart your moment, Skye. I wasn't going to say anything today. But then you pitched that one about being pregnant right over the plate, and I couldn't help but swing."

"Are you freaking kidding me right now? Batter up, sister! If you hadn't told me? I would've been so mad at you!" I gave her another quick squeeze. "If I had sat here and gone on about my city hall drama and you had awesome news like that? Growing right there in your belly?" I put my hands over my mouth as the gravity of the moment really started to strangle me.

"What's wrong? Skye? What is it?" Laura looked genuinely concerned.

"There's a baby—inside your body. You're going to be a mama," I whispered.

"No. It's very important we don't get confused. I mean, I had to go through countless hours of counseling, and part of that was learning how to talk to others around me about the process of being a surrogate." Laura launched into a spiel, and I cut her off at the pass.

"Okay. Cut the bullshit, hon. This is *me*. I know the process. I know it's not really your baby. I know Mona and Roger made the baby batter and put it in your oven to bake. I understand science." I rolled my eyes and took a swig of my beer. "It doesn't change the fact that there's a baby growing inside you. You're going to feel it moving and growing and changing your body. That experience will be yours and yours alone."

She let a huge smile spread across her entire face and sat there for a few moments. "All right, let's shift gears, though. This is getting way too heavy. We can do this in a few months when my hormones are out of control." My friend ran her finger through the condensation on her glass. "I already miss beer," she said wistfully.

I pushed my glass toward her. "I'm pretty sure you're allowed to have a drink now and then."

"Nah, it's not worth it. I've seen what my sister and her husband have gone through to make this happen. I would never knowingly do anything to endanger this baby. As strange as this will sound, I can already see why mothers go off the deep end the way they do when their kid is in danger. And this little bean is barely a thing. I can't imagine what it's like when they're three or twelve, or shit—twenty-two, you know?"

"Wow." It was all I could say.

"What?" my friend asked.

"Just, wow," I repeated. All it took was a single moment in time for a person to change completely. The change could be good, the change could be bad, but the change happened. In the blink of an eye, the world as we knew it became something altogether different. In response, everything around the person who changed also changed. A chain reaction—a domino effect.

What did all that mean? My decision became clear in that very moment. It might have sounded melodramatic or scripted like a TV drama playing out in my head. But it was the truth. It was time to make a change, to *be* that change. Our city was struggling on the inside. The citizens didn't even know half of what was going on inside city hall. But it was time to make a difference. To make our city a place that we were all proud of again. A place where young parents, like Mona and Roger, wanted to raise their children. A place where people felt safe and happy and could prosper.

"So, I've decided to run for city council," I blurted without preamble, and Laura almost choked on her Sprite.

"When did you decide this?" she asked once she'd cleared her throat.

"Just now," I said nonchalantly, baiting her for a reaction.

"Isn't that something one typically gives a little more thought to? I mean, what happened to the city manager idea? Actually, hold that thought. I need to find a restroom. I'll be right back."

I watched her walk away until I could no longer see her figure across the room. She didn't look any different, and I thought to myself how silly that was to even be thinking. What did I expect to see? A neon sign above her head blinking the words *baby on board?*

Telling Laura I had just decided to run for city council wasn't the whole truth. Sure, I'd finalized my decision at that moment, but I'd been working toward the goal my entire life up to that moment. But like the final piece of a puzzle clicking into place, Laura's decision to help her sister start a family made my path clear as well. I wanted to use my political voice to make our city the place families grew and prospered again. The place we were all proud to call home.

"Skye Delaney?" asked a deep male voice. "Hey, I thought that was you. How have you been?" A familiar-looking guy perched his ass on the stool Laura had vacated.

"Do we know each other?" I knew exactly who the guy was, but I wasn't about to give him the satisfaction of knowing I remembered his name.

"Aww, come on. You remember me. Kyle Armstrong? UCLA Constitutional Law major, like you." He winked and gave me a lazy grin. If I hadn't already disliked him, it might have been a little sexy.

Fine, a lot sexy.

Squinting my eyes, I gave him an obvious once-over from head to toe. "Hmmm, doesn't ring a bell." Truth be told, I could pick this guy out of eight hundred others. He was a smug prick who always rubbed me the wrong way. Typical entitled socialite, Southern California born and raised, silver spoon in one hand, BMW keys in the other. List a spoiled-brat stereotype, he checked the box. The exact type of guy your mother warned you about.

Or encouraged you to marry.

On a few occasions, I could've sworn I'd seen him around the small café on the corner by my office. A lot of people who worked at city hall ate lunch there or popped in for a quick cup of coffee before heading to the office for the day. The guy had very remarkable eyes, the sort of feature you couldn't help but notice. I'd remembered them from our school days, so when I'd seen him at the café, I was almost sure it was the same guy. This run-in confirmed it.

"I think you're being coy. I was in Sigma Nu. Surely you partied at our house? I mean, everyone did, right?" He laughed like we shared some inside joke, which we didn't.

"So, is there something I can help you with, Carl?"

"Kyle."

"Right, sorry. Kyle." I purposefully didn't sound apologetic. At all.

"So, what are you up to now?" He leaned his arm on the table, and I couldn't help but notice the way each individual muscle was defined in his forearm.

"Hmmm—what? Sorry?" When I looked up to his face, he was grinning.

Cocky jackass.

"Listen, it's been a very long week at the office. I met my friend here to unwind a little bit, so if you wouldn't mind—I mean, it was nice seeing you again and all—"

Our waitress approached the table and set a cocktail

napkin down in front of Kyle. I quickly picked it up and handed it back to her. "Oh, no, he's not staying. Thank you, though." I gave her a look like *help a sister out,* and she gave me a knowing smile in return.

"Can we get four Cîroc shots, lemon wedges on the side? Thanks, Chrystal." He had the balls to take several cocktail napkins off her tray while he was talking and set one down in front of me, one down in front of himself, and one down in front of the empty barstool where presumably Laura would be sitting when she returned from the restroom.

"On my tab, please," he called to Chrystal as she sauntered away.

She gave a little wave over her shoulder in acknowledgment.

"What exactly do you think you're doing?" I looked at him and then the napkins, flabbergasted.

"Helping you unwind a little bit. That's what friends are for, am I right?" he asked, flashing that sexy grin again.

"But we aren't friends. I don't even know you," I answered tersely.

"But you will." His voice dropped a notch, making my stomach flip-flop in response.

Oh, no, we are not going there. Not with this one.

I slid Laura's napkin back to him. "She's pregnant." Maybe that wasn't my news to share, but he already had me a bit off-kilter.

He took that same napkin and slid it across the table to me, holding eye contact with me the entire time. "More for you and me, then."

"Are you trying to get me drunk?" I tilted my head a bit in a challenge.

"Will it increase my chances of you coming home with me?" He raised one eyebrow suggestively.

I stared at him in disbelief. With the timing of a saint, Laura came back to the table, taking the vacant stool closer to me since the one she had been sitting on was now occupied by Kyle.

"Hi, I'm Kyle. Laura, right?" He extended his hand, and they shook in a friendly way.

"Yeah, hi. You look familiar. Have we met before?" She looked at me, and I shrugged my shoulders. I had already had it with this guy, so she was on her own.

Chrystal returned, her tray lined with shot glasses full of clear liquor, a bowl of lemon wedges in the center.

"Oh, boy, what's this?" Laura asked, looking at me again.

I motioned across the table with my chin, placing the blame squarely where it belonged.

Kyle, having no sense of customer/server boundaries, began unloading the shot glasses off Chrystal's tray, placing two in front of me and two in front of himself. The waitress, finally allowed to do her freaking job, placed the bowl of lemon wedges between the two of us.

Laura watched the whole thing in silence, although I could tell she was holding back a fit of laughter.

"Anything else?" She automatically deferred to the jackass, and at that point, I didn't blame her. He would probably wrestle her to the ground for her order pad otherwise.

Thoughts of wrestling on the ground with that hard body pinning me down made me squirm in my seat a little bit.

"You okay over there?" my *former* friend Laura asked as

heat crept up my neck and made my face flush. Why she felt the need to point it out, I wasn't quite sure.

"Yeah, it's just getting a little hot here. I noticed it last time too." Total lie, but no one had to know that.

"Let's have a toast, then. To new friends." Kyle held a shot glass up in the air, and Laura followed suit with her freshly refilled Sprite. Although I wanted to knock the glass out of Kyle's hand, I raised my shot glass instead, and we all met in the middle to clink together and hail "cheers."

I tossed the vodka down, set my shot glass on the table, and reached for a lemon wedge at the same time Kyle did. Our hands locked on each other instead of the citrus, and I sputtered and coughed as the burning fire of the liquor etched the lining of my throat. He moved his hand to pat my back, and I yanked myself out of his reach, grabbing a lemon and sucking quickly to counterbalance the effects of the vodka.

"I didn't peg you for a rookie." He chuckled.

"Oh, dude, noooo." Laura cradled her face in her hands, shaking her head from side to side. "Don't poke the beast."

Kyle laughed harder. "Is all of that supposed to mean something?"

"No, never mind her. Let's have this other shot so you'll go away." I picked up a lemon first this time and the shot glass in the other hand. "Bottoms up!"

"Wait!"

I looked at him impatiently.

"What about a toast?" he asked.

"Go for it," I said with zero emotion.

"To the baby." He held the shot glass toward Laura.

The mere mention of the baby softened my ire instantly. I guessed babies really did have magical powers. I swiveled toward Laura as well, holding my glass aloft.

"Yes, to the sweet, sweet baby. But more importantly, to the oven it's baking in. I love you."

"I love you too," my girlfriend said, and I hopped off my stool to give her a quick hug before we clinked our glasses together, ignoring Kyle completely.

"Hey! Don't forget about me. It's bad luck to miss someone in a toast."

"For Christ's sake, this guy," I mumbled under my breath but loud enough for Laura to hear.

She was laughing behind her hand as she stretched across the table to touch her drink to Kyle's. I did the same after her, locking eyes with him over the small glasses.

He stared at me. Like really stared. Not at me—into me. He was ridiculously good-looking, but his eyes were a conundrum, a confusing puzzle of the light spectrum, and it wasn't because of the shitty illumination inside Itza's. His irises were an amazing amber color that I'd honestly only seen in felines before. The pupils were large—in this case, the credit did go to the crappy lighting of the bar—but the stark contrast to the gold made them seem even bigger and the white on the outside even whiter.

His hair was another mystery. Not that I'd spent a whole lot of time looking at the man since we'd been sitting at the table. But I couldn't decide if it was brown or possibly red. Kyle was a pretty animated guy, with tons of energy, who seemed to enjoy chatting it up with people. It would take pinning him down long enough to really study the thick waves. I mean really run my fingers through to his scalp to feel the glossy depth to understand what color it truly was.

There was that nagging inclination again. That of pinning him down, being pinned down.

Being restrained. Wrestled. Spanked.

Punished.

God. It had been so long.

Too long.

"Skye!" Laura shouted my name over the din of the growing crowd, trying to get my attention.

Shit. "What?" I shouted back, probably louder than necessary. *Sorry,* I mouthed to her. She could read me like a book, and the grin painted on her face told me she had my number already. I closed my eyes for a few beats, sucked in a deep, hopefully calming breath through my flared nostrils, and opened my eyes again to find her still staring—still grinning.

"I'm going to get going, babe. I'm tired, and my back is starting to bother me from this stool. Just a little preview of what's to come, I guess." She slid off her seat, and I gave her a hug.

"I'm going to head out too," I said to her. "We can finish the conversation we started before we got company another time. But soon, okay? I'd really like your input. Time is of the essence, as you can imagine."

Laura twisted her face in thought. "Yeah, that confuses me a bit, actually."

"Not here. Call me tomorrow, maybe on the commute. You'll have to take a day off from your audiobook, though." I loved teasing her about her secret romance novel addiction.

"I don't know... Things are starting to heat up. I'll see what I can do." She hugged me again, and I held on extra tight.

"I'm so proud of you. You are the most selfless person I know. I could take a few lessons from your book." I stood back, still holding her hands as we inched away from each other.

"Be a good girl," Laura commanded as we let go of each other's hands.

"Never," I called to her back as she left the bar. It had been our ritual goodbye since our college days. I watched her get into her car, parked right out front. She had the best parking spot guardian angel in the city. I, on the other hand, always had to hoof it three blocks in the shitty neighborhood direction.

I had completely forgotten about Kyle, who took me by surprise when I turned back to the table to grab my bag. I jumped a bit when I saw him still sitting there, watching my private moment with my friend.

"You're still here? Really?"

"That was really sweet. The two of you like that." He motioned to the door.

"So glad you approve. Hey, thanks for the shots. I'm taking off. Work and all. Peace. Out." I tossed a ten-dollar bill on the table for Chrystal and turned to leave.

"Why don't I walk you to your car?" In my peripheral view, I saw him adding more cash to the money I'd put on the table. Fury burned inside, but I wasn't about to get into it with the guy and prolong our association.

"Not necessary," I snapped and started toward the door. He was nearly jogging after me to keep up with my purposeful stride, and it was a little embarrassing—for him, I mean.

I was out on the sidewalk and around the corner, heading in the direction of my car, and I could still hear the patter of his steps following me.

"Skye, hold up. Slow down. Let me walk with you."

"I said no thank you. I'm right up here. Just go back to your buddies."

"I'd much rather talk to a beautiful woman than those Neanderthals any day."

"Do your guy pals know you have terms of endearment for them like that?" The entire conversation was going on with me shouting over my shoulder while power-walking to keep a decent distance between us. His clap backs were coming on his rhythmic exhales. He had the measured breathing of a toned athlete.

"The sad thing is they probably wouldn't even know what the word means." His quick-witted tone was absent. "They would think it was a European sports team or a video game at best."

That caught me off guard, and I stopped and turned to look at him. He used my pause to his advantage and quickly closed the gap between us, and I realized my mistake too late. Now we stood toe-to-toe on the dark corner of a residential side street.

"You shouldn't park this far away when you're alone. It's dangerous." He stood so close, I could feel his breath on my skin.

"What if I told you I'm packing heat?" I decided to challenge him just for the hell of it.

"I wouldn't doubt it for a second. And I'd be substantially aroused," he answered, unaffected by the idea of a weapon on my person.

I leaned back to take an obvious look at his crotch. Indeed, he was.

"You're a ballsy lady. I like it," he said after passing my inspection with flying colors.

"It's not a concern of mine. I'm just another block," I said, motioning in the direction of my car with a tilt of my head. "You should go back. I can handle myself."

I turned to leave, but he grabbed my wrist and yanked me back toward him so forcefully that we made a *thunk* sound when our bodies collided.

"Oh, danger, Will Robinson. What do you think you're doing?" I spoke the words of protest but made no actual motion to pull away. None. At all.

"Kissing you. For starters." His low voice seemed to drop further.

"So presumptuous," I whispered, using the last bit of oxygen I had.

Kyle smashed his mouth to mine. Nothing fancy. No finesse. Just lips, tongue, sucking, thrusting, grinding, mashing, melting.

Moaning.

Jesus Christ, this guy could kiss. Not the pansy-ass bullshit I had dealt with in the recent past. Which, if I were being honest, had turned me off from dating completely. I was worried for the entire male gender after the last string of dates I'd been on and how they had kissed. But not this one. My faith was rekindled with one freaking kiss.

I dug my fingers into the fabric of his shirt to hold myself steady while he stole my sense of balance. The world tilted on its axis just a bit more when he pulled back and stared at me with those crazy cat eyes of his. Before diving in for another taste, he teased me. First by licking and nibbling the outside of my mouth, kissing my jaw and neck, and then returning back to my lips. Just when I thought I'd get the full action again, he moved away and traveled along the other side of my face. Then he progressed to my ear and earlobe, where he sank his teeth into the fleshy part and quickly soothed the pain away with more sucking and licking.

"Oh shit. Stop. Enough of this bullshit. Yeah. No. This stops here, big man." I shook my head to clear the fog he'd induced with that magical, sinful mouth and tongue of his.

His eyes, even though heavy-lidded, glowed in the dimly lit night. "Let's not stop. Come home with me. Or take me to your place. Either one. Just don't stop this. It's way too good." His chest pumped with every inhalation.

Even his voice had taken a different edge that was hard to resist. Deeper, scratchier. Drawing me in with invisible strings pulling directly on my pussy. He reached for me again, and I swatted at his hands. "No. That's exactly why we aren't doing this."

"That doesn't make sense. Why deny yourself something that feels good? That's what life is supposed to be about. Living. *Feeling*."

"No," I said immediately. "That's what gets you in trouble in life. Those are things that lead you off the path you're focused on. Temptation leads unto evil. Haven't you ever been to church? That's all they ever talk about in those places."

He laughed deep in his throat, and *fuck me* if that wasn't alluring too.

"Who are you?" I shook my head and stepped away from him. "For real, who are you? And where did you come from? You show up here tonight, a place I always hang out. You know my name. You know my friend's name. Where I went to school. What gives?" Suspicion was my middle name. Well, after Control Freak and Neat Freak, according to my former roommate, Oliver.

"You know who I am. You know you've disliked me since we were in poly-sci, sophomore year." Kyle took a step toward me, but I held my ground.

He didn't intimidate me. Quite the opposite, actually. I was inexplicably attracted to him. I wanted to drop to my knees and suck him off in the middle of the street.

His nostrils flared as if he had read my last thought, and he came closer still, dropping his voice to a near whisper. "You can't stand the fact that your pussy is throbbing for me right now. It's a hard pill to swallow for a woman like you. I get that, Skye, I do. Wait till my cock is in you so deep and you're screaming my name. You think that kissing was hot?" He completely invaded my personal space and pressed his chest against mine. "Girl, you don't even know. Wait till you can't get me out of here." He tapped my temple and then slid his hand back under my hair, grabbed a handful at my nape, and tugged my head back. I had no choice but to stare up at him.

I did nothing to fight him off because, whether it was right or wrong, I liked what he was doing. I liked what he was saying. He was one hundred percent right. My panties were so wet they were sticking to the lips of my pussy as I stood there in the middle of the street, craning my neck to stare up into his glowing amber eyes.

"You need the kind of man who's going to take you in hand. I can tell from that bratty mouth and sexy strong will of yours. Not change you. Embrace and appreciate you," he said and then pulled back. "I'm going to say good night, even though I'm going to have to beat off three times before bed, thinking about you. But when I call you tomorrow, pick up. Now go home and get some sleep. Stress isn't good for anyone."

"You don't have my number," I said.

How that was the thing that came out of my mouth, I would never know. Why my brain chose that moment to be practical was the mystery of the month.

"Of course I do."

He leaned down and kissed me. Still demanding and in control, still skilled and intoxicating, but this time there was a quiet carefulness instead of the chaotic storm of before. My head swam from the endorphins my body had released from being at his mercy, and when he stood me on my own and moved away from me, I felt the loss immediately. A part of me wanted to renege and invite him home, but my rational side was stronger, and I dutifully dug for my keys instead.

"Bye. I guess?" It was all I could come up with.

"Pick up when I call tomorrow," he said, pushing his hands deep into his pockets and watching me walk the rest of the way to my car.

"Oh. Okay," I said, walking backward so I could see him. "We'll see how that goes." I grinned, testing him already.

He made a face that confused me, so I quickly turned and headed toward my car without saying another word.

It looked like he was disappointed with my answer, and for some reason that made me feel...*bad*. That was where the confusion set in. How, within a couple of kisses, did a relative stranger change my mindset? I definitely needed to have a stern talk with myself on the drive home. There wasn't a penis on the planet worth giving up myself for.

Hell no.

I'd worked too long and too hard to be derailed now.

CHAPTER THREE

The next morning, I couldn't wait to get on the road so I could call Laura. She picked up after the second ring.

"Boy, you weren't kidding. I didn't even get to hear three sentences of my audiobook before my phone rang." She ended her comment with a big yawn.

"Am I already boring you?" I teased my friend.

"No, I haven't been sleeping well. There are already a million things running through my head about this pregnancy. I don't want to mess it up."

It was strange to hear Laura doubt herself. She was one of the most confident women I knew. When I wasn't sure how to handle myself in a situation, I asked myself, *What would Laura do*? It was a strategy that had helped me through quite a few pickles.

"You need to stop this. You're going to be amazing. And the really good thing? Your body knows what to do all by itself," I told her. "Nature designed us that way. You live a healthy lifestyle already, you eat well, you're in great shape. This is going to be a piece of cake. Stop worrying." I hoped she could hear my heart in the pep talk.

"Thank you, Skye. I really needed to hear all that this morning." She sighed. "There's so much extra pressure because it's my sister, you know? They want this baby so badly, and there were only three viable embryos. They only implanted one, so we were lucky it took."

"See? My point exactly. This was meant to be. It's going to be fine." I slammed on my brakes because traffic slowed unexpectedly. "What is this? We just randomly stopped for no reason. I don't have time for this bullshit this morning."

"Settle down, Danica. It opens back up. Every morning it slows down in the same spot. You know this." Laura was on the same freeway that I was, a few miles ahead. "So, finish your story about what has made you decide to run for city council. No better yet, who was that Kyle guy?" Her voice perked up considerably. "Did he just walk up and start talking to you?"

I was hoping she wouldn't bring him up, but he definitely was the more interesting topic of conversation. Now I had to decide how much detail to get into with her. As much as I loved my friend, there were a lot of things she didn't understand about me. My needs and desires in the bedroom being number one on that list.

"Do you remember him? From UCLA?" I asked her.

"He looked familiar, but I couldn't really place him. Did you date him?" she asked.

"Hell no. I couldn't stand the sight of him. Apparently some things never change," I said, stretching my neck and looking ahead to see why the traffic was stopped.

"Oh, I wouldn't say that," said Laura.

"What is that supposed to mean?" I stared at my phone as if she could see the look I was giving her.

"Are you kidding me right now?"

"No, what do you mean?"

"The two of you were looking at each other like you wanted to eat each other up."

"Oh, give me a break," I snapped. "I think your hormones are already screwing with you. He's an arrogant asshole."

"Just your type." She laughed.

"I don't like assholes!" Maybe I protested a little too much.

"Oh, my God, Skye! You're like an asshole magnet. You always have been. It's that smart mouth of yours. They're drawn to it like a moth to a flame. I think guys like him see you as a challenge." Leave it to Laura to call it like she sees it.

"You air-quoted *challenge*, didn't you?" I could totally picture her making the hand gesture while she was driving.

She burst out laughing, her husky chuckle filling my car and making me smile. "Yeah, I did. You know me so well. And I know you so well." The line went quiet for a moment, then she asked, "Did you go home with that guy?"

"No. Please!" I snapped again. Maybe I needed to lay off the caffeine a bit. "Like I said, he's an arrogant asshole."

"So, you made out with him, then?"

"Laura, seriously." I was so busted.

"That's a yes." Again, she just let dead air prepare me for what she would ask next. "Well?" she finally blurted when I didn't offer details.

"Well, what?" My patience was wearing thin.

But if I did a little self-examination regarding the anxiety and frustration I was feeling, it had nothing to do with Laura's curiosity. I was so mixed up about how I really felt about what happened on that dimly lit street the previous night.

"Was it awesome? I mean, he is stunning. Those eyes. I don't think I've seen anything like them."

"I know, right? And it was *ridiculous*. Like capital R, ridiculous. It was very hard to walk away and drive home alone." There. I said it.

"Why did you? You've had quite a long dry spell." Blunt Laura, as always.

"I don't need the complication right now," I told her. "I'm about to launch the first campaign of my career. I'm not going to have time to water my plants, let alone get into a new relationship. The last thing I need is some needy guy getting butt-hurt every time I show up late for a date or don't return his call. And those things will end up happening in the middle of a campaign."

"Sounds like you have it all figured out, then," she said.

"Is that supposed to mean something?" Damn, I was always so suspicious.

"Nothing more than what I said."

There were a few beats of silence before she followed with another question. "So where did you leave things?"

"Well, there weren't really things to leave. We made out in the middle of the street like two drunk people do. Although neither of us was drunk. Not even buzzed, actually. But regardless, yeah. No *things* to leave. I can't imagine I'll hear from him again. I didn't give him my number."

That was the complete truth. Whether he said he had my number or not, that was another story. But Laura didn't need to know that. Whether I actually hoped he would call or not—

well, Laura didn't need to know that either.

"All right, my little kitten. My boss is on the other line, so I've got to go. I'll get with you later. Have a good day. Play nice with the other kitties." Then she was gone.

My car was suddenly quiet—just me and my racing thoughts. Traffic was a damn nightmare into the downtown corridor. By the time I got to my desk, I was ten minutes late. Being late was one of my biggest pet peeves. I nagged my coworkers about it constantly, so when I was the one who was tardy, they pounced like tigers on fresh meat.

Tara hit me first as I came around the corner into our stall. "It's not like you to be late. Did your watch stop?" She had a snide little grin on her face, as if she had just scored a three-pointer.

"You're right, it isn't like me at all, and I'm disgusted with myself. Traffic was a real bear this morning coming in from the west. I guess if I lived by the rest of you guys, I would've missed that mess on the 101 East." Dramatically shuddering, I added, "But that would mean I lived in the valley, so yeah, no thanks." That was probably the nastiest thing I'd said to someone all week, but it wiped the smirk off her face in seconds. If she hadn't laid into me the moment I walked through the door, she could've saved herself from my forked tongue.

The first thing on my agenda for the day, outside of my normal workday routine, was to get in touch with Bailey. If I was going to run for city council, I would need her help and in a big way. I had to be very careful about what communications I sent on my city-owned computer, so starting that morning, I brought my personal laptop with me and opened it on my desk alongside my work computer. I needed to multitask at all times to maximize my workday, and I needed to warm up to the idea of late work nights and very little social life for the next few weeks.

I texted Bailey from my own phone and asked her to call me when she had a chance. My phone rang within minutes, and I answered quickly so I wouldn't attract too much attention from the people in the office.

"Hey, thanks for getting back to me so quickly," I said in a quiet but conversational tone.

I probably should've looked at the caller ID first. It wasn't Bailey's voice that responded to my greeting.

"Anyone who leaves you waiting is a fool," a masculine voice answered.

"I was expecting another call. Obviously."

"Sorry to disappoint you."

"Don't be. It happens a lot. Can I help you with something? I'm at work." I really needed to set this guy straight from the get-go. He couldn't just call me and think I'd go all giggly and mushy at the sound of his voice.

"I just wanted to say good morning and that I hope you have a productive day."

"How Hallmark of you. You can text that next time. I'm super busy. Talk to you later." I disconnected without giving him a chance to say anything else. I wanted to free up the line for Bailey, who coincidentally called within the next minute.

"Hey there. Thanks for calling me back." This time I was sure to have checked the caller ID, so I knew I had the right person.

"Yeah, no worries. I take it you've come to a decision?" Bailey was a straight-to-the-point kind of woman like me, and I appreciated that.

"I have. I'm going to do it." I looked around my small office, making sure my pen mates were busy with other things besides eavesdropping on my call before continuing. "City Council, I mean." I sat back in my chair and grinned. I let the weight of my decision really settle through my bones.

"Good for you, Skye. I think it's a great first campaign. You may even win." She paused only a second or two before firing a litany of questions. "Have you given thought to what your infrastructure will look like? Have you filed? What about your public announcement? Where are we at?"

"I have some of these things ironed out, but I was hoping you might want to help me?" I spoke in a rush, trying to convince her. "You'd make a perfect campaign manager. You've done it before for William. You know this city inside and out."

Nervously, I waited for her answer.

"You're right, I have done it before," she said. "And you're right, I do know this city inside and out. But there's a problem. I think having me as your campaign manager will hurt you."

"Why would you say that?" I wasn't following her line of thought.

"Simple," she said. "I have a giant target on my back right now. Many people are out of jobs because of what I did. Don't get me wrong... I don't regret one second of it. But I don't want you to be unfairly judged because of your association with me. And it will happen, Skye, trust me."

"I see where you're coming from." Of course, it was

obvious now that she'd said it. "Damn. You'd be perfect. I'm not sure who else I have in my stable."

"Well, that doesn't mean I can't help you," she said, cutting through my grumbling. "I need to be a behind-the-scenes girl. For starters, maybe website design, database, donations, social media management, and advertising. That should keep things running, at least in the beginning. You will have an abbreviated campaign as it is, so there are a bunch of usual steps that will be skipped altogether." Now Bailey was off and running.

She would definitely be my campaign manager, but not in the public eye.

"While I have you, Oliver wanted me to invite you over for dinner tonight. He said to tell you he's cooking one of your favorites. Are you available? Could you come over right after work?"

"I would love that," I said. "I can't believe I'm going to admit this out loud, but I'm getting a little tired of Cocoa Puffs. How about if I text you guys when I leave the office?" I was already excited about the idea of eating a home-cooked meal.

"That sounds perfect. I'll see you later. Oh, and Skye?"

"Yeah?"

"Congratulations. You only have your first time once. Try to savor the moment."

"Thanks, Bailey." I ended the call and sat back in my chair. The weight of my decision was really beginning to settle on my chest, and it felt like an enormous elephant had pulled up and popped a squat. It already explained why so many elected officials within the office had bottles of liquor stashed in their desk drawers.

"Everything okay?" Tara interrupted my wayward thoughts.

"Yep, good as gold here. Why? What's up?" I asked, sitting up taller in my chair.

"Nothing. You just looked a million miles away." She shrugged while answering.

"Oh." I faked a laugh and waved my hand toward my cell phone lying conspicuously on top of my paperwork. "My mom. She calls at the worst times. You know how moms are." I rolled my eyes dramatically, apparently satisfying her curiosity, though, because she moved on to the next peer to nose her way into their activities.

The midday news made the election postponement their lead story, and pundits began speculating what that meant for the City of Angels. For the first time in our history, an election was rescheduled due to a large percentage of the candidates dropping out of the race. The new election would be held in one month. Interested parties had until midweek the following week to file their forms with the city clerk. Since special circumstances were in effect, the normal time parameters for filing were being waived for all positions holding elections. I couldn't remember the last time I'd heard a call for candidates on the mainstream news. If ever.

By the end of the workday, I managed to complete all the filing documents without anyone in my workspace suspecting a thing. I typically kept to myself during the workday, finding tasks to do even if there wasn't obvious work set in front of me. Lately, with so many of the higher-ups missing in action, the gaps were getting wider and wider.

I created an organized spreadsheet of other documents I needed to gather from my home office, copy, notarize, and include with my filing package in the morning.

For a mental reprieve, I worked on a press release, officially announcing my candidacy for Los Angeles City Council. I would run it by Bailey tonight after dinner, and together we would come up with a timeline for my campaign in general.

The day flew by, and before I knew it, everyone was saying goodbye to me while I was still hunched over my laptop. I had worked straight through lunch, stopping twice throughout the entire day to pee and refresh my iced tea. My eyes were so strained and dry, I felt like I'd been on the back of a horse galloping through the Mohave.

What was I even saying? I'd never ridden a horse in my life. And had zero desire to do so.

Checking my phone for the time, I saw a screen full of notifications.

"Oh shit. What's all this?" I scrolled while shutting down my laptop.

Two text messages were from Laura checking to see how my day was going. Nothing unusual there—we often said hi or shared a joke or funny meme throughout the day.

Apparently I'd missed a phone call from my mom, but she hadn't left a voicemail. Again, nothing unusual there, as she always said she hated talking to machines. I'd have to give her a call on my way to Oliver's—the universe's way of punishing me for lying to Tara earlier, saying I'd been talking to her.

Two missed phone calls were from a number I didn't have

in my contacts. The calls came about thirty minutes apart, but the caller hadn't left a voicemail.

The last notification was a text message, and when I looked closer, I realized it was from the same phone number as the two missed calls.

You're supposed to pick up when I call.

Well, that explains whose number kept showing up on my screen.

How do I deal with this guy?

I selected one of the phone calls and added Kyle to my contacts. That way when he called again—because I had a feeling he would—his name would show up on my display.

If that kiss hadn't kept barging its way into my thoughts all day, making it difficult to concentrate on matters at hand, the answer would be easy. Then there was the way he'd pulled my head back by a fistful of my hair—as if he had every right to do so—and how that action had called to a very dark place inside me. A place very few people even knew about, yet Kyle Armstrong had zeroed right in on it.

Yeah. All of that. If all of that didn't exist, the answer would be easy. However, all of that *did* exist. Not only did it exist, it was screaming at me from the front row, center stage. *Hey, lady! Remember me? Your sad and lonely libido? The thing that's been so bored and fed up with these schmucks you've brought around here lately? Remember me?*

I waited for the elevator to stop on my floor. The second wave of people was leaving for the day. Not the employees who lived and died by the clock—the ones who never stayed a second past quitting time. These were the folks who stayed to get the job done but knew where to draw the line. You wouldn't catch me sleeping on a sofa in my office like I'd seen William do on more than one occasion.

When the elevator door opened, the car was pretty full. "Room for one more?" I squeaked. Even though there was some grumbling in the back, a few people up front shuffled closer together, and I stepped on board. The man standing closest to the number panel made eye contact with me. "Parking," I said. "Looks like you have it already, thanks."

I busied myself with sending a text back to Kyle.

I didn't agree to such a plan. Did I?

When I hit Send, my phone made the *whoosh* sound to signal a text was on its way through cyberspace to find its lucky recipient.

Toward the back of the elevator, someone's phone signaled, almost with perfect timing, that they received a message. Probably a notification of an email or a social media post. It could've been anything. It was the timing that I found entertaining.

I stuffed my phone in the pocket of my coat and stood aside as a few people disembarked on the next floor down. When my phone chimed again, I reached back in my pocket to silence the thing. The phone's repeated chirping in this confined space was probably annoying the other riders, and it was a long ride stopping at every floor on the way down to underground parking. I stole a glance at my screen and saw another text from Kyle, however, so I checked his message.

Your hair looks good like that.
Shows off the sexy line of your neck.

I froze with my hand hovering over the reply option. How did he know how I'd worn my hair today? He had to be the other phone I heard chiming in response to mine in the elevator. What were the odds of him being on the same elevator I was on?

The city hall building in Los Angeles was a behemoth. While it was originally built in the late nineteen twenties, it had been updated many times and stood proudly, an iconic part of the city's landscape. Thirty floors towered into the bright blue Southern California sky and provided workspace for many of the city's nearly thirty-five thousand employees. The chances he and I both worked for the city were still slim, considering there were over four million people living here. Extrapolating the odds that we would both be in the same elevator in the same building at the same time? Well, that would require the aid of a rocket scientist or two.

Regardless, my body seemed to be the water to his divining rod. My pulse spiked immediately with his nearness. My breathing accelerated as I thought of the previous night coupled with the text I had just read.

He thinks I look sexy?

If I turned around to search the sardines stuffed in the tin can of the elevator, he would—without a doubt—be wearing that damn smug grin of his, and I would be four shades of embarrassed that he saw the effect he had on me. If I texted him back and he hadn't silenced his phone, all the other elevator riders would figure out we were texting each other.

My phone vibrated in my hand while I was trying to figure out my next move, catching me off guard and making me jump a little. I heard his muffled chuckle from deep in the back of the crowd. I decided no matter what floor we stopped on next, I was getting off.

As if on cue, the elevator slowed at the second floor and the doors slid open. I stepped off quickly, but whoever had called for the elevator originally on that floor was nowhere to be found. The man at the control panel hit the button to close the doors so they could be on their way, but a long arm sliced its way between the two closing halves, halting their progress. A bunch of grumbling sounds came from inside the car as the doors slid open again. Kyle stepped out and straightened his suit jacket, smoothing the material down flat and adjusting his tie.

"You're a slippery one, Ms. Delaney," he said.

"Me?" I asked incredulously. "This from the guy stalking me at my place of employment." Goddammit, he looked amazing in a suit. The slacks fit him to a T, and the burgundy tie he wore played with the red hue in his dark hair.

"Maybe you're the one stalking *me* at *my* place of employment?" He sauntered over to where I leaned against the wall of the atrium.

The autumn sun was fighting for its life in the evening sky, and the harvest colors added to the confusion of his actual hair color.

"I really do like your hair like that, though," he said. "It's making it very hard not to touch you right now." He looked around as if assessing the danger quotient of a public display of affection in the middle of a hallway in a building that, apparently, we both worked in.

"Are you fucking stoned?" I gaped at him, both for the way he shifted subjects and because he looked completely edible at the moment.

"Pardon?" He looked back at me quickly, as if I'd interrupted his risk assessment.

"You wouldn't have the right to touch me, no matter where we were standing." I softened my tone completely. "Thank you, by the way. I was just trying something different." I made an awkward motion toward the hair that had come loose from my updo and was now hanging at my nape.

"Do you really work in this building? Here at city hall?" He leaned against the wall with one shoulder and looked down at me. Even with my pumps on, he was still a few inches taller.

"No. I was just riding the elevator up and down a few times for a cheap thrill. We don't have those fancy things where I come from." What could he possibly think I was doing in this building on a weeknight, exactly at quitting time, with a briefcase and a handbag dangling from my shoulder?

Kyle shook his head slowly from side to side. "My God, you're a handful. So refreshing. Let's try this a different way. See if you can manage an appropriate response to *something*." He stood up straight from the wall and dramatically adjusted his posture and suit. He reached into the pocket on the inside of his coat and pulled out his business card.

Extending his hand in greeting, he said, "Hello. I'm Kyle Armstrong. I work in the assistant district attorney's office, specifically in special operations as the grand jury advisor."

I shook his hand and took the little card as a slow smile spread across my lips. This guy was too much, and I realized Bailey was spot-on with her opinion of my poker face. It sucked.

"Well, it's nice to meet you, Grand Jury Advisor Armstrong," I replied. "I'm Skye Delaney. I, too, work in this old pile of bricks and mortar. Just a few floors up in the mayor's office. I'm the assistant to the city manager."

"Impressive, Ms. Delaney. No wonder you have such a bad attitude all the time."

"I beg your pardon?" I looked up from his card, which I had been studying so I wouldn't be staring at his gorgeous face.

"Well, working for those old buzzards can't be very much fun. At least until recently, with all the drama you've had up there," he added.

"Well, I go to work to get my job done, not to have fun. But as *fun* as this little run-in has been, I need to be off. I'm meeting someone." I walked toward the elevator to press the call button, and he stepped in front of me, blocking my path.

I looked up at him impatiently.

"You're meeting someone? Tonight?" His voice took a darker tone where it had just been playful moments before.

"That's what I just said. I would think if it's your job to deal with grand juries, you'd pay closer attention when people speak. No?" I stretched around his tight backside to press the button, but he wouldn't budge. "Move your ass so I'm not late."

He stepped to the side, and I pressed the down arrow.

"Why don't I go with you?" he asked hopefully.

"For starters, you haven't been invited. Secondly, I'd like to enjoy my evening. And you, Mr. Assistant District Attorney slash special ops slash grand jury advisor, are a giant pain in my ass."

Untrue on so many levels.

In some unexpected combination of moves, he spun me around and caged me between his long arms and the frame of the elevator, giving me nowhere to move except against his firm—*and Christ, I mean really firm*—body.

"Dude. No way." I tried pushing on his chest, but it was like pushing on a brick wall. "You can't do this shit here. We both work here," I whispered loudly in case anyone came around the corner to use the elevator.

"You're making me act irrationally. I don't know what you're doing to me, but I know I don't want you to walk away from me again right now," he said, leaning in closer. The faint scent of his cologne still lingered on his skin, teasing my senses with an exotic blend of spices.

"Haven't you learned by this point in life that you don't always get what you want?" I finally summoned enough courage to look up into his eyes. I had them imprinted in my memory from the night before, and they were still every bit as mesmerizing.

"Are you going out with another man tonight?" His tone dropped to an edgy, serious one.

"Yes. There will be a man there." No need to explain my relationship with Oliver. "But again, I need to point out how none of this is your concern."

"I can't let you go." He folded his fit arms across his chest, and I quickly moved away from him.

"Do you hear yourself? We met last night. We made out in the middle of the street. We didn't elope. Get a grip, my friend." I was a little bit unhinged after being so close to that freaking body again.

"I can't deal with you being with another guy. I haven't had a chance to...to—"

"Jesus Christ, do I even want to hear how you finish that sentence? What? Skin me alive and wear my flesh as a double-breasted dinner jacket?" I asked, my voice rising in volume and intent. "Or—or keep my severed head in your freezer?"

Thankfully we must have been the only ones left on the floor, because no one had come to the elevator the entire time we'd been standing here. I leaned against the wall again where this whole ridiculous conversation started. My equilibrium was way off-kilter.

He chuckled. "You've been watching too many *CSI* episodes. I was going to say I haven't had a chance to properly take you out." He took two steps toward me, and I froze. His amber eyes zeroed in on mine, keeping me in place while he spoke.

"Or make you dinner." This time his voice was quieter, deeper. Two more steps and he was pressing up against me.

Him.

Against me.

Against the wall.

"And then fuck you." His voice was somewhere between

a scratch and a scrape. The only difference between the two being one leaves a mark while the other doesn't. This would definitely stick with me for a while. Likely until he made good on his words and the promising look that came along with them. Both of which had wetness rushing to my pussy like I hadn't felt in months.

Many, many months.

Kyle pressed his lips to the hollow just below my ear. That perfect, sensitive spot that made the hair on my arms stand on end and sent a tingling sensation down my spine to dance across my clit.

"You want that too," he grated beside my ear before nibbling the lobe.

"You don't know what I want," I panted.

He slid his hand into the opening of my trench coat and thumbed my hard nipple through the thin fabric of my blouse. He leaned back to watch my response while doing so. I closed my eyes to hide from my traitorous body's affirmation.

"Stop lying to yourself. And to me. It doesn't suit you," Kyle said so close to my lips I felt his breath on mine while he spoke.

Those were the last words I heard before I kissed him. I couldn't deny myself another chance at what I experienced the night before. Just one more time before I officially declared him a no-fly zone. Now that I knew he worked within the same building—shit, just about the same department—there was no way this could go on. I wouldn't screw up my future over a piece of ass.

That ass, though.

My God. I reached around and dug my fingers into his cheeks so I could have the tactile knowledge to complete my fantasy. I needed to know how that tight, not-too-round, not-too-flat, perfect male rear end felt beneath my hands. Now when I pleasured myself, I would remember how it felt to have my nails sunk into his flesh, so I could imagine gripping him and pulling him into me while he fucked me.

"Mmmm," he groaned as he thrust his tongue deeper into my mouth. And now I could imagine it would be the same with his cock. Deeper and then deeper still.

I moaned in response, wanting to hike my leg up on his hip so he could grind his hard cock against me. Forget the fact that we were still against the wall in the second-floor atrium of city hall—both our minds were in a far better place.

Abruptly, he pulled back, panting. "Come home with me."

"No. I can't. I told you, I have plans," I said, sucking in a deep breath and then straightening my clothes.

"Cancel them," he said sternly, grabbing my hands away from my busy work. "Seriously. Cancel. Them. I have to have you."

"Not tonight, Chief. This date is too important. Besides, this whole thing"—I motioned back and forth between the two of us—"is a bad, bad idea. Capital B bad. You know it as well as I do."

"It doesn't feel bad to me. It feels like the complete opposite of bad, actually."

I strode over and pressed the call button for the elevator. Because I had called for it before, it was still on our floor. The bell dinged, the doors slid open, and I quickly stepped into the car. I hurried to press the button for them to close before he could say or do anything to stop it. The panels slid shut, keeping me from going home with him because, God help me, I was about eight seconds away from doing it.

Smashing the P for the parking garage, I tapped my toe impatiently while the car descended. When I got to the bottom level, I pressed all the buttons to send the elevator on a wild goose chase to at least ten other floors before it could return back to the garage level with Kyle on board.

Then I all but sprinted to my car so he wouldn't see me when he finally did get off the elevator after me. He already knew what car I drove from the night before, so hiding from him was out of the question. My only hope was to be in my car and driving away by the time he got down to the parking deck. My tires squealed as I pulled out onto the street from the building, and I hit the phone icon on my steering wheel and brought up Oliver's name on the display.

"Hey, Skye Blue. Are you on your way?" My dear friend's voice eased my nerves right away.

"Yeah, finally. Sorry, I was...uh...held up, I guess." I huffed.

"You guess?" he teased. Oliver always loved juicy gossip—a vice he developed from his years in the fashion industry, hanging around the other catty models.

"Long story." Hopefully if I kept my response brief, it would quell his interest.

"Oooh. Sounds promising! Can't wait to hear all about it," Oliver said in a sing-song voice.

Or not.

"You wish. Anyway, do you need me to pick anything up?

Traffic looks pretty light, I should be there in like...fifteen?"

"Nope, we're all set here. Just need you. Bailey's printing some stuff off the internet, but she won't tell me what it's all about. Said you should break the news to me, so I can't wait till you get here."

"All right, I'll see you soon." I smiled as if he could see me. His excitement was so endearing.

"'Kay, drive safe."

"Bye, Ollie."

We hung up, and I drove the rest of the way in silence. So help me God, if Kyle called or texted me tonight, I was blocking his number. It was going to be my only hope of resisting him. Getting involved with him, on any level, would be career suicide. Politics and relationships with others in politics went together like lemon juice and milk.

Eewwww. But that was the general idea. They didn't go together at all.

I put some music on, and by the time I pulled up in front of Bailey and Oliver's house, I was belting my heart out with Bruno Mars to his dirty anthem "Gorilla." Which perfectly fit my mood after the experience with Kyle.

Time to switch gears, though. I had a campaign to organize and a potential campaign manager to convince she was the right woman for the job. Even if it would be a behind-the-scenes, you-do-all-the-work-and-get-none-of-the-credit type scenario. Who wouldn't jump at that opportunity?

CHAPTER FOUR

When you're as tired as I was when I left Oliver and Bailey's later that night, the shortest drive home seems like a cross-country trek. Even the idea of walking from my car to my front door had me thinking about laying the car seat back and sleeping there. Although I lived in a decent neighborhood, the sketchiness factor had me dragging my bum up the sidewalk, despite how exhausted I was.

My zombie-like state was worth it, however. The night with Bailey had been very productive, and I was proud to say I officially had a behind-the-scenes campaign manager. Oliver was one hundred percent supportive of both of us, which was important given the amount of time we were going to be spending on campaigning in the upcoming weeks. We had a very tight timeline to work with because the election had been rescheduled for exactly four weeks from that night. There was no time to flounder with decision-making. Things had to move at a breakneck pace, and Bailey's experience was going to be invaluable.

We had agreed to meet at the city clerk's office in the morning to file the paperwork confirming my intention to run for city council for the seventh district of the City of Los Angeles. Since candidates were required to be residents of the district they represented, it was destiny that the mayor pro tem was the current city council member from my district.

If he announced a candidacy for mayor, that city council seat would be empty, and my campaign would begin. We would know his intentions within the next few days, and life as I knew it could change for good.

Bailey had told me over dinner she still had a few friends on the inside at city hall. They would serve us well over the next few weeks as we strategized. At that point, no other candidates had been into the city clerk's office to file for the vacant city council seat.

I filled in the last few blanks on the forms after my third cup of coffee. Even though I should've been wired for sound, I could barely keep my eyes open. I had to hunt in my home safe for documents I hadn't seen in years, finally finding them buried underneath mementos and other nonsense. I stuffed everything back into the vault, promising myself to clean that mess out at my first free moment.

Ha! Who the hell knew when that would be?

My cell phone vibrated on my nightstand where it was already charging. Like most people, I had the same routine every night, and charging my phone while I slept was at the top of that list.

I squinted my tired eyes at the screen and immediately regretted looking. *Fucking Golden Eyes.*

Can't sleep. You up?

What to do, what to do? If I engaged him at this hour,

I would never get rid of him. But in my weakened state of exhaustion, I could admit to myself there was a slight chance I didn't really want to get rid of him.

A very slight chance.

One message couldn't hurt. Really, how much more damage could it do? When the sun came up, he was off-limits. That was my final answer.

No rest for the wicked.

The bubble popped up right away to indicate he was responding.

You're not really wicked. That's just
what you want people to think.
Nice trick with the elevator btw.

Are you sure I'm not wicked?

I can handle you. More than one way to skin a cat.
Make that pussy.

Wow. That's where you went?

Go out with me.

You can't just demand things like that.

Sure I can.

Things are going to be really busy
at work for me for a while.

All work and no play...

Night.

See you tomorrow.

Doubtful

;)

I turned off my light and fell asleep almost instantly. Odd dreams had me tossing and turning all night: My mother disapproving of me running for office. Bailey quitting halfway through the campaign because she said I was going to lose and she didn't associate with losers. Oliver telling me he never wanted to see me again. And the final straw that had me waking up in a cold sweat... Laura gave birth to a bouncing baby porcupine, and when I went to congratulate her and the father, Kyle stood by her side, beaming with pride.

Okay, what the hell was any of that?

Luckily it was close to the time my alarm was due to buzz,

so I shut it off and trudged to the kitchen for a cup of steaming jet fuel before hitting the shower. Listening to the local news channel while I got ready gave me a jump on what I would face when I got to the office. As predicted, Mayor Pro Tem Jack Carter had announced his bid for mayor, thus vacating his seat on the city council. I finished doing my makeup with a shit-eating grin on my face and texted Bailey with the news. Of course she had already heard and was sending me a congratulatory text at the same exact time.

We decided that, since she wanted to stay out of the public eye as much as possible, I would go file my paperwork on my own. My announcement would be made later in the day, and that, too, was something I would do solo. There really wasn't a need for her to be there, and it wasn't something a campaign manager typically took part in. Bailey had enough things on her to-do list from the night before to keep her busy for a week of Sundays.

Instead of going straight to the office, I called ahead and talked to Tara. There still hadn't been any mention of who would be handling the city manager position, and now that MPT Carter was going to be busy with his own campaign, I didn't expect he would be around the office nearly as much.

"What's the temperature like around there?" I asked Tara when I got her on the line while driving to work.

"What do you mean?" she asked, confused. "I don't know, like normal? Mid-seventies, I guess? You know, someone always turns the air conditioning down when Carter's not around, and then we all freeze. Did you forget a sweater again?"

Holy shit, is she an airhead.

"I meant, what's the mood like, Tara? Since Carter announced he's running for mayor this morning, I figured everyone would be either really happy or really annoyed."

"He did what? Are you serious?" Her voice rose to such a high pitch I thought my eardrums were going to burst.

"Do you even listen to the news? Or own a television?" If I didn't know better, I would think I was talking to a thirteen-year-old.

"Not usually. I mean, yeah, I own a TV, but my boyfriend is usually watching UFC or football. When I get in the car, I just want to listen to music, you know? Sing along to some Justin Bieber. Oh, my God, he's so hot! Have you seen those underwear ads he did? Seriously..."

Between the Valley girl sing-song quality of her voice and the subject matter in general, I was pretty sure someone had to be playing a prank. How could she be a work peer of mine?

"Okay, I need to do one thing downstairs at the clerk's office before I come up, so I may be a bit late getting to my desk," I said. "Not that I think anyone will miss me, but in case someone comes by looking for me, I'm on my way, okay?"

"No worries, Skye. I've got it covered," she answered way too cheerfully.

"Thanks, T. I owe you one." I ended the call as I reached the street of my building. I parked in the auxiliary lot to avoid any off chance of running into Kyle in the parking garage. Eventually I wouldn't have to play games like these, but the idea of "us" had to get a few layers of dust on it first. For him *and* me.

The city clerk's window had no line. It may have been

the first time I'd ever seen it so empty. I was so giddy with excitement I nearly dropped the thick folder as I took it from my briefcase and set it on the ledge.

This was really about to happen. All the years of hard work. All the planning, all the studying in school, all came down to this moment. My first campaign started right here.

"Good morning, Shelly. How's it going this morning?" I said to the friendly face on the other side.

"Hey, Skye, no complaints. How are you this fine day?" Her warm smile was always genuine and pleasant.

"Pretty good. No complaints from this end either. I'm calling that a win so far." Shelly and I had both worked in this building for years. We'd gotten friendly at office functions, all-hands meetings, and simply passing in the halls. She was a lovely woman, very smart and very good at her job. She always had a happy demeanor when I saw her, and I appreciated that in a place where so many people seemed so sour all the time.

"Well, what can I do for you this morning?" she asked. "I'm not sure I've had the pleasure of helping you at my window before." Her pen was poised.

"Actually, I'm submitting all this." I pushed the thick folder under the plexiglass divider. "I want to run for the city council seat for District Seven."

"Well I'll be. Congratulations. Someone's finally going to put her brain to good use instead of chasing behind some monkey's ass for a living." She smiled brightly and then quickly mumbled, "No offense."

"None taken." I chuckled at her comment. "You know we all have to climb the ladder, Shelly, one rung at a time.

Sometimes you get on the ladder behind a monkey. That's just the way it works out." I shrugged, knowing darn well what people had thought about William Hardin long before he died and all of his wrongdoings came to the surface.

"Girl, don't I know it. Don't I know it. They're slippin' on banana peels in here, left and right."

I barked in laughter and quickly tried to disguise it as a cough behind my fist. "Oh, pardon me. Gosh, excuse me. I hope I'm not coming down with something." I bugged my eyes out at her, and she silently laughed, her whole upper body shaking as she did so.

"You're going to get me in trouble, Ms. Delaney," she said conversationally, as if she were talking to me about my paperwork. She was quick on the uptake—if we caught anyone's attention, it would seem like we were having a regular conversation.

"Me? You're the comedian here," I said in the same tone.

"Listen, I know you need to get up to work. I'll run through all this, and if anything needs fixing, I'll give you a holler, okay?"

"Oh, you are the best. Thank you so much." I closed my briefcase while we finished up.

"And Skye? Best of luck. You'll be great at whatever you do." Her sincere wishes made my day.

"Thanks, Shelly. I'll come down at lunch and pick up my original documents," I said, planning out loud, not wanting to leave any of those things behind.

"Perfect."

When I left the small room, a few others had begun to form a line, confirming I had gotten there at the perfect time.

The morning flew by in the office, as I had so many fires to put out, thanks to Carter making his intentions public. People were mainly concerned that the duties of the mayor would not be handled while he was on the campaign trail, so I set up a meeting with the current press secretary to review the official talking points on the matter. It was a legitimate concern for citizens and deserved a well-coordinated answer.

An enormous bouquet of my favorite flower, gladiolas, stood on my desk like tall spires of different colors. Only Oliver would know both my favorite flower and that I had something to celebrate. He was truly the best man who ever walked the planet. Always so thoughtful, and he always went out of his way to make my day special.

"These are amazing, Skye. What's the occasion?" Tara asked as I sat down at my desk, beaming at the arrangement.

"Oh, my bestie, Oliver. He's the nicest human on the planet."

"Uhhh, I don't know about that." She plucked the card from the pick that held it in the bouquet and squinted at the writing. "This definitely doesn't say Oliver. I mean, it's typical guy chicken scratch, but definitely not Oliver." She stretched around the flower spears to hand me the note.

"What the fuck? How the hell..." I didn't want Tara sniffing around this juicy story, even a little bit.

Congratulations on your candidacy.
May the best man (or woman) win.
Can't wait to see you tonight.

Kyle

So many questions ran through my head, I couldn't decide which one to address first. Probably the most important: how did he know I was running for city council? Only four people knew, and three of them wouldn't tell if their lives depended on it. That only left Shelly. Guess I was taking a little field trip to pick up my documents. I should've done it at lunch like I said I was going to, but I'd lost track of time and hadn't gotten to it.

"Tara, I need to run down to the clerk's window. I'll be back in a few minutes. I'll take my cell phone in case you need me."

"No problem," she called over her shoulder, absent-mindedly scrolling through her Facebook feed. It was likely she didn't absorb a word I said.

On my way downstairs, I tried to figure out the answers to the less important question. How did he know my favorite flower? Maybe I had posted that somewhere on a social media quiz or something. I was about to dismantle all those accounts before my public announcement anyway. Could never be too careful.

I popped my head into Shelly's office, or room, as it really was.

"Oh hey, girl, here's your stuff. Sorry I missed you at lunch. It's been swamped all day. You have a knack for hitting at the right time, both times today."

"Actually, I was tied up at lunch and wasn't able to come by, so I guess it all worked out. Hey, can I ask you something?" I looked around again to make sure no one had walked in.

"Sure, anything. Your paperwork looked great, by the way. Unlike the other guy. He had to redo a few things two or three times. It was kind of entertaining actually."

"That's just what I was going to ask. Have others filed today?"

"Yep. Looks like two others for District Seven," she said and referred to a clipboard she had beside her. "Someone by the name of Lloyd Jessup, and also Kyle Armstrong."

I banged my head playfully on the wall beside her window.

"Hey now, don't be breaking things out there by my window. Especially body parts. I'm not staying late to clean up blood. Not today, girlfriend," she joked.

"Yeah, this day just got really interesting for me too." I took a big inhale and let my shoulders drop down. "Okay, thank you again for all of this." I held up the documents. "Let me know if I can ever be of service to you, my friend."

"I'm going to hold you to that," she replied, pointing at me through the glass pane.

"I hope you do."

I spun on my heel and headed back up to my office. While in the elevator, I pulled out my phone and sent the stalker a text.

Thank you for the flowers.

You're welcome. Pick you up at seven for dinner.

Can't. Busy.

Then I'll meet you at your place after.

I was getting furious with his insistence. What was it going to take for him to get the hint? And now, to top it all off, he was running against me for the same city council seat? The only city council seat that was open? I was typing feverishly on my phone when the elevator stopped at my floor, and I stepped out without looking up and plowed right into the solid wall of a man.

"Goddammit," I mumbled to myself. I was about to apologize until I saw it was Kyle.

"Do you ever actually sit at your desk throughout the day? This is the third time I've come by, and you've been out every time. That girl in your office is starting to give me the creeps with the way she eye fucks me." He stared down at me while he spoke, as if reprimanding me.

"You should ask her out," I said. "You'd stand a better chance with her. And some of us work around here. Crazy, I know." I held my hand up to stop him from speaking. "You can't keep coming around here. It's going to give people the wrong impression."

"And what would that be?" challenged Kyle, who began to back me up toward the wall until I realized what he was doing and held my ground.

"That we have any sort of association, relationship, friendship, anything at all"—I paused but then added for more effect—"whatsoever."

"So, the flowers were too much?" he asked, almost as if I hadn't said a word.

I shrugged. "Well, they are beautiful. And they are my favorite. How you knew that is a bit concerning." My ire slowly returned as I spoke. "I'm choosing to leave that stone unturned. Kyle, seriously." I leaned in closer, and he did the same, and I could tell it was only to be closer to me and not to listen to my quiet tone. "If we're opponents in a political race, let go of the idea that there could be any sort of anything between us. It's never going to happen. Nothing. Ever. I mean, you get that, right?"

He looked around the elevator atrium quickly, making sure no one was near, and then he bent forward to speak directly in my ear. Damn this man and his knowledge of my hot spots. "That's exactly why we should have a proper farewell tonight. After this, it's going to be every man for himself."

Goosebumps broke out across my arms and on my thighs. Before I could respond, he was walking over to the elevator and pushing the call button, hopefully returning to his office and leaving me alone.

"Think about it. And your ass looks stellar in those slacks" was all he said as the door closed, his cocky grin the last thing I saw. I wanted to slide to the floor in that very spot and kick and scream in frustration, but instead I stretched my neck to each side for a few long seconds and power-walked back to my stall.

Tara, with her uncanny ability to ask dumb questions at the exact wrong time, nailed me as I walked into the room.

"So, who's the guy?" She tried to act innocent, but with two kids at home from two different baby daddies and no ring on her finger, innocent wasn't a word that best described her.

Looking around the room, I asked, "What guy?"

"Nice try, Skye. This one," she said and motioned toward the flowers. "What was his name? Collin?" She went for the card, and I snatched it from her reach and stuffed it in the pocket of my pants.

"Yeah. Collin. He's just a guy from a bar the other night. But you know how it is. He's way more interested than I am. I don't know how to get rid of him now."

"Oh, stage-five clinger," she said and rolled her eyes in commiseration. "The worst."

"You don't even know the half of it." I tried to busy myself at my computer, hoping she'd take the hint and do the same.

"But who's the guy that keeps sniffing around here? He's been in here at least three times today. Hot as hell too," she said, eager to know more. "If you're not going to jump on that, sister friend, throw a girl a bone. Or boner, if you hear what I'm sayin'." Tara burst into a fit of giggles at her own crass joke. Really, it wasn't that funny.

I looked up from my monitor. "I thought you were going to finally settle down with the boyfriend? The baby's father? You said that yesterday in the break room."

"Hey, just because a girl is on a diet doesn't mean she can't look at the menu." She finally went to sit at her own desk and get some work done, or her version of work, which meant looking at her Instagram feed. Which was fine by me because she stopped talking to me—and talking about Kyle.

After clearing my email inbox, I called Bailey to check in. "Hey there. How's your day going?"

"Not bad. Getting a lot accomplished. How about you? Did you file with the city clerk?" Bailey got right to the point, as usual. I would never mistake a conversation with her for anything other than work.

"Yes, ma'am. First thing this morning. Uh, found out some interesting news." I dropped my voice. "Looks like I'll be having some company. Two others." I tried to keep my conversation vague in case Tara was eavesdropping. It was a terrible habit of hers, and while I didn't expect her to know what I was talking about, crazier things had happened.

"Well, I would've been more surprised if you were running unopposed, to be honest," said Bailey. "This is where a lot of people interested in public office get their feet wet. Probably the only thing keeping the field small is the tight timeline."

"So, what's on the agenda for tonight? Are we getting together?" I asked. I assumed we were and was more or less checking out the details.

"I promised Oliver we'd go on a date tonight," she said. "We had a long talk last night after you left, and he understands that you and I will be seeing more of each other over the next month than he and I will. We're going to spend the night making up for that ahead of time." I could hear the anticipation in her voice as she spoke.

"Enough said. Please, details aren't necessary. Especially for the girl whose dry spell has been longer than the California drought." I groaned.

"Maybe you should go out yourself. We're going to be pulling some late nights, Skye, and you're going to have less than no free time. I'm not exaggerating."

"Point taken," I said. "Honestly, if I had someone to call, I'd consider it. I think I'll pamper myself with a nice hot bath and a good book. Just some good old-fashioned *me* time."

"Whatever suits you. Hey, I wanted to ask you. Do you have any vacation days saved up?"

"Yeah, a ton. No offense, but your husband worked me like a dog. If I ever asked for time off, he said no." No sense beating around the bush as to why I never took time off.

"You don't have to keep saying 'no offense' every time you speak William's name." She laughed. "He was a bastard. I know that better than anyone. I taught him everything he knew. Well, except for all the corruption and cheating and lying. He figured all that out on his own. But he was a hard worker, and he expected the same thing from those who worked for him. Just like I do."

"Again, point taken. Okay, have fun tonight, and I'll see if I can get some time off around here. I'm thinking closer to the election would be best?" I asked to be clear.

"How much time do you have? Can you take the entire month?" Bailey asked.

"I have the time, but I doubt it would be approved," I told her. "Literally no one is in this office right now. Now that Carter will be campaigning too, I'm not sure who's running the show. He has a few assistants in his office who are about to get some serious on-the-job training. I almost wish I was in that spot at the moment." It wasn't a lie. Those staffers were being thrown into the fire, feet first.

"I get your point, but you need to focus on this campaign, so don't get any crazy ideas about helping them out. Do you hear me?" Bailey's manner shifted to a mentor's warning.

"Of course. Don't worry. I have my priorities straight. Talk to you tomorrow. I'll polish my announcement tonight, and we can blast it in the morning instead of this afternoon."

"Perfect. You took the words right out of my mouth. Okay then, have a great night, with your book or whatever." She chuckled.

We hung up, and I sat back in my chair. Now that I really didn't have plans for the night, the giant floral arrangement was taunting me. Possibilities poked at me like the spears of buds shooting from the glass container.

Seeing him would be a very bad idea.

Very. Bad.

But sometimes, being bad was the exact reason something was so good. I thought about it off and on for the last hour of the workday, and when quitting time came, I rushed out of the building as if it were on fire. If I saw Kyle on the way out, I wouldn't be responsible for my decision. I was having a full-scale war with myself as it was.

The drive home was unbearable. By the time I pulled into my condo complex, I had made up my mind and changed it again three different times. While I was tormenting myself, I filled my bathtub to the very top with lavender-scented bubbles and then soaked away my self-induced tension.

When the water was too cool to enjoy any longer, I rinsed off and got out. I flopped onto my bed to drown in the silence of the condo. Normally I preferred to be alone, but something about the quiet was deafening tonight. No, not just the quiet—everything. I strolled out into the living room while I towel-dried my hair, where even the furniture seemed to taunt me.

In the kitchen, my lone cereal bowl and spoon sat in the

drain rack, reminding me how long it had been since I had thrown a dinner party. Just another token of the amount of time that had passed since my place had been filled with the sounds of laughter and storytelling as friends caught up with one another over a shared meal.

I shook my lonely thoughts away and wandered back to my room, telling myself I'd been too busy for those things lately. But I knew that wasn't what was really bothering me.

The truth was, I didn't want to be by myself at the moment. I wanted to feel desired. I wanted to feel alive. To feel the thrill of doing something I shouldn't. And the prospect of it being within my reach was making me want it even more. Just days before, when there was no possibility of the temptation of hooking up with a mouthwatering, deliriously sexy man, I had all but forgotten about sex. I'd been perfectly content.

But now, Kyle Armstrong was under my skin. Burrowed into my frontal lobe like a worm. Just like he'd predicted he would be. I already hated the bastard. I had hated him in college for his looks and his arrogance, and the hatred was growing by the moment. I stared at my phone lying on the bed beside me, dark screen taunting me. All it would take was one simple text.

One message.

One invitation.

One night.

I typed the message and left it on the screen without sending it. I gave myself the chance to beat it to death in my brain just a bit longer. Why not overthink it? That was how I went through my entire life, after all. Measured steps, careful plans. Everything in its proper place.

Fuck it.

8732 Wyngate 91040

For several minutes the message went unread, and panic set in. Now, of all times, he wasn't going to immediately respond? Was he kidding? Every other message I had ever sent him, no matter what time of day it had been, was immediately read and answered. If two more minutes passed and he didn't respond, I would follow up with an *oops, wrong window* cover-up. Even if he saw right through it, at least it would cancel the invitation.

I set the timer on my phone and stared at the seconds ticking by. One minute and forty-two seconds remained.

The signal strength at the top of the screen showed four bars. Just like it always did everywhere inside my home. That wasn't the problem.

One minute left.

I was one minute away from having made one of the most embarrassing mistakes of my adult life.

There was no way I could stare at the timer for another sixty seconds. I stormed into the bathroom and brushed my teeth. Extra vigorously because plaque had nothing on me at that moment. Next, I moisturized my entire body with my favorite lotion, hoping the calming scent would take me to a serene island with gentle waves lapping at my ankles, like the picture on the bottle promised.

It didn't.

Back in my bedroom, I picked up my phone, sure that the

timer had run out and I'd be doing damage control. I opened the screen with the facial recognition feature and heaved in a breath of air so hard I choked on the saliva that flew down my throat with it.

Jesus, I was acting like a high schooler. But I was giddy with excitement and relieved beyond measure all at the same time. I had to flop onto my bed to get my shit together.

All I could do was stare at the screen. This was really about to go down.

Be there in twenty.

CHAPTER FIVE

Deciding to keep it casual, I threw on a pair of yoga pants and a long-sleeve T-shirt. There were no delusions about what was going to happen tonight, so I couldn't see the point of getting all dolled up. If all went according to the fantasy in my head, I'd be naked within a few minutes of him arriving, we'd have ridiculous animal sex for an hour or two, and then he would leave.

Your basic booty call, just like it was meant to be.

A quiet knock on the front door spiked my pulse. Even though I was pacing back and forth right in front of the thing, I counted to fifteen before I opened it. Didn't want to seem too eager.

"Hey. Glad you found the place all right." I stood to the side so he could come in and then quickly closed the door. Neighbors were friendly in the complex but could also be a bit chatty. After my announcement tomorrow, I'd have no privacy whatsoever.

"I actually live near here. Same district, obviously. I'm glad you changed your mind about getting together. Should I ask what prompted the change of heart?"

"Let's just say a friend shared some words of wisdom," I said with a sly smile.

"Was this the girl you share an office with? I'm not sure I'd use the word 'wisdom' in the same sentence with that one," he said. He looked at me skeptically but playfully.

I had to laugh, as his assessment of Tara was spot-on. "No, definitely not. I wouldn't take advice from her if my life depended on it."

We were lingering in the entryway. I wasn't sure if I should show him to my bedroom or sit on the sofa. What was the correct protocol for a planned night of sex?

"Can I get you something to drink? Or eat? Although I doubt there's much here in the way of actual food." I walked toward the kitchen, just to do something other than stand by the front door. If there were a candle inspired by the mood in the room, it would be called Awkward Moments.

"What do you eat if there's no food here?" he asked, following right behind me.

"I'm a big fan of cereal. Cocoa Puffs, mainly. I dabble in Raisin Bran and the occasional Cocoa Krispies."

"I sense a cereal theme here."

"Guilty as charged." I stopped with my hand on the refrigerator door handle to find him right behind me, trapping me between the appliance and his tall frame.

"You'd make a terrible criminal," he said. "You're not supposed to admit guilt that quickly." He put his hands on the top of the refrigerator, caging me with his firm chest against mine so I could feel his voice vibrate through me when he spoke. I had to tilt my head back significantly to account for our height difference. Because I was just wearing socks and every time I had seen him previously I was wearing heels of some sort, I really got a clear idea of how stark that difference was. At least eight inches, I would guess.

"Christ, you're tall," I said, looking way up to his handsome face.

"Six-foot-two. I'm guessing you're about five-four, maybe five-foot-five?" he said, pressing farther into me. I felt his erection between us.

"Yeah" was all I could think to say, and I was pretty sure that was his intention by the smirk on his lips.

"We should talk about a few things before you show me your bedroom."

"Oh? What kind of things?" I was hoping cocky Kyle was going to come out to play.

"What you like, what you don't like. Are there things that freak you out? Stuff like that." He pushed a few strands of hair back from my face while he spoke. His fingers felt like they were charged with electricity, creating a low hum on my skin when he touched me.

I needed to keep this light, at all costs. "Dude. We're not getting married. We're going to fuck. One and done. We don't really need to tell each other our deepest darkest, do we?"

"The way I do things, we do."

"How do I even respond to that?" I said. "What does that mean? The way you *do* things. Do you *do* things in such a different way? Like how many ways are there to *do* what we're going to *do*?" Antagonizing him was quickly becoming a favorite hobby.

"If you haven't noticed, I lean toward the dominant side of things." He trailed his index finger along my jaw. "If that's a problem for you, you need to speak up now. It's the way I prefer things in bed, but it's not a deal breaker for me. If you allow me to have control of your pleasure, it will be the best experience of your life. That, I can absolutely guarantee. If you prefer nice, gentle, vanilla sex, I can do that too. It's just not the way I'm wired." The way he was pressing his cock into my belly while he was talking was distracting me from his well-thought-out speech, but I caught most of what he was saying.

I thought about his words for a few beats before answering. I completely understood what he was saying, and I had read enough books and watched enough porn to know what he was talking about.

"The other night, in the street? The way you kissed me? The way you pulled my hair?"

"Yes?"

"I want that. I want the full version of that. However you want to describe that, sign me up." I looked directly into his mesmerizing eyes so he would know I meant what I was saying.

"How do you feel about being restrained?" He ran his index finger under the neckline of my T-shirt. How that became erotic, I had no idea, but I was so amped up, I felt tingles in my sex from the simplest touch.

"In theory, it's exciting and a really hot idea." My voice wavered when I spoke, and I felt so silly. It was like going to second base behind the dugout in junior high. "Although, practically speaking, probably not so great on the first time I'm with someone," I babbled while he trailed his finger across my neck a few more times and then back up to my jaw. "I don't really know you, so that should make perfect sense to you. You know the statistics as well as I do."

"All right, I can understand that. Spanking?"

"Christ, we just dove right down some kinky rabbit hole, didn't we?" I said weakly.

"It's better if we talk about it now, rather than in the middle of doing it and you don't like something I do to you," he said, like he'd said it many times before. He knew exactly what he was doing. "Don't you agree?"

"Yeah, I see your point. It's just crazy we're having this conversation. I'll never be able to get something out of my refrigerator again and not think about this moment."

"I told you before, I'd get into here." He tapped my temple like he had when we first met, warning me he'd get inside my head and it would be difficult to get him out. Little did he know I was already past that point.

After a few moments of me staring into his golden eyes, he said, "Spanking?"

I shook my head slightly, trying to clear my thoughts. I really wanted to kiss him and get on with it. Enough with the negotiations already. Maybe it was the lawyer in him that had this strange need to hash out all the details of everything before he went through with something.

"Can we just kiss now? I don't want to talk anymore." My voice cracked on the last word because my throat had gone so dry from the need building inside. "Please."

"So sweet to hear you say that." He bent toward my mouth, and just before touching my lips he said, very softly, "Say it again, Skye. Say it with my name."

I looked up at him through my half-closed eyes, lashes

fluttering to fan my desire. "Kyle, please," I whispered. "Please kiss me." I let my eyes close slowly and waited to feel his mouth on mine.

My reward was the storm I'd felt the first time he'd kissed me. A full, powerful onslaught of firm lips, with his one hand wrapped around the back of my neck to hold me in place, the other hand at my throat to ensure I complied. While his tongue explored deep inside my mouth, I gripped on to his forearms to steady myself, for my balance was affected by the sensation overload. He mixed the kissing with short breaks where he would apply slight pressure to my throat or tug my hair tighter around his fingers behind my head. There was always something happening, keeping me on alert. This was the furthest thing from predictable or mundane. It was, by far, the best kiss of my entire life.

When we parted after several minutes, I was a breathless, needy, hot mess. Stripping down to my birthday suit and fucking on the kitchen floor sounded like a perfectly reasonable option, and I was a nanosecond from suggesting it when he broke into my chaotic thoughts.

"Where's your bedroom?" He stepped back to allow me to lead the way. I guessed the bed did sound better than the hard tile floor when enough oxygen circulated to my brain to form a coherent thought.

"I'll show you." I extended my hand so I could escort him down the short hall to my room. I'd made sure things were tidy before he came over, and my housekeeper had just changed the sheets that morning, so the timing of the booty call couldn't have been better from a house-proud standpoint.

"This is a really nice place. I can appreciate the minimalist decorating style. Reminds me of my own place, actually," he said while grinning. "Do you have a roommate?" he asked when we walked past Oliver's old room.

"No. I used to," I said. "But he moved in with his lady love, so now I'm here by myself. I guess I'm in the market for a new one, but I haven't been trying too hard. I've been enjoying the solitude, if I'm being honest." I was rambling. Nerves had a way of doing that to me.

"I get that, but the rent's got to be pretty steep. And now you're financing a campaign too?" he asked, maybe also nervously rambling.

"Definitely don't want to talk about any of that right now," I said, backing up until the back of my knees hit the edge of my bed.

"Oh, let me get the lights. One sec." I went to move past him to turn out the lights at the wall switch by the door.

"Leave them on." His gravelly voice was low and commanding.

I went to protest, but the look on his face made me stop in my tracks.

Shit.

Not to mention feeling like I might have an orgasm where I stood. *Christ, what is that all about?* Over leaving the lights on? Did this guy have some sort of magic spell cast over me?

"Uh...okay," was the best I could come up with. I watched him close the space between us in one purposeful stride and come to stand in front of me in the center of my room.

"Put your arms above your head," he said without

emotion. A simple statement. Not a request, not a smile or a friendly suggestion.

Nonetheless, my arms went up, as if I were reaching for the stars. Kyle skated his fingers around the hem of my T-shirt, just skimming my bare midriff where the shirt rode up because of my arm position. Luckily I wasn't ticklish, or I'd be doubled over from the contact.

My shirt was up and over my head and in a pile on the floor before I could think about anything else. When I dropped my arms, he looked at me, head tilted to the side slightly, a disapproving vibe souring the air. I quickly raised my arms up over my head again, mentally comparing our exchange to a grown-up version of Mother May I?

"Quick learner. I like that." As a reward, instead of one jump and one skip toward Mother, Kyle took off his shirt too. He was very toned but not too bulky, which I appreciated. He took excellent care of his body, and it showed.

He walked behind me and stood so close, we were skin-to-skin. He ran his fingers from my wrists down to the sensitive underside of my arms and then continued all the way down to my armpits and along the side of my breasts. My nipples peaked in response to his touch, straining against the satin cups of my bra. He repeated the motion several times and then moved my hair completely to one side, exposing my neck and shoulder on the other.

Clearly we were both quick studies, because he had learned my neck and ears were erogenous zones on our first encounter, and he always returned for more when given the chance.

Zero complaints from this girl.

Kyle unfastened my bra but left it in place. He kissed my neck, starting just behind my ear and working his way down to my shoulder. While his mouth was busy with the kisses and nibbles, he slid his hands from my waist upward, skating across my ribcage and the delicate underside of my breasts. Heat rose between my legs as he petted and toyed with my flesh, bringing me more and more pleasure with simple touches and kisses.

My nipples ached, they were straining so tightly, begging to be pinched or plucked, bitten or sucked. Something to relieve the tension that had gathered at the firm points. As if he could understand my need, he cupped my breasts, one in each large hand, and fondled them roughly.

I leaned my head back onto his chest and moaned. Wrapping my arms around his neck, I pushed my breasts farther into his hands. "Is this okay? My arms here?" I figured I'd better ask, rather than get *the look* again. Or, God forbid, have him stop doing what he was doing.

"It's perfect. You're perfect just like this," he said quietly in my ear.

"Feels so good. Soooo good," I moaned.

He rolled my nipples between his fingers, softly at first, then adding more pressure when I didn't protest.

"Do you like that?" he goaded.

"Yes."

"More?" he asked while adding more pressure to my tight tips.

"Mmmmm." I pressed my ass back into his hard cock.

"Say yes if you mean yes, Skye Rocket."

I grinned. No one had ever used that one before. "That's definitely a first."

"Rocket? Just a promise of things to come." He pressed down on my nipple, and I moaned loudly. I felt a rush of wetness between my legs.

"God. I could come just from you doing that. Feels so good."

"Really? Let's see if that's true, shall we? Come over here." He towed me over to the bed, where he sat on the edge and positioned me standing between his legs. My tits lined up right in front of his face.

"I've fantasized about this." He looked up at me with those amber eyes while licking around my nipple with his wickedly skillful tongue.

"So have I," I admitted. "Real life is so much better." I couldn't take my eyes off what he was doing. It added to the tight feeling building deep in my stomach. "Can I touch you?"

"Of course you can," he said before going to work on the underside of my breast, one of my favorite places on my body to have kissed and licked, even bitten.

I dug my fingers into his hair while he worked at my breast, driving me higher and higher with each lick and suck.

"Bite me," I whispered, looking down at him.

He raised an eyebrow, and I knew I shouldn't be telling him what to do. I quickly tried to defend myself.

"How else will you know what I like? You said it yourself. I'm so close to coming." I whispered the last part. Then waited. "What if I say please?"

"That might make it okay." He grinned around the

mouthful of breast he'd just devoured.

So while he was in the perfect spot, I said in a low, throaty moan, "Kyle, please, bite me, right there, yeahhhh, oh God, yes! Yes!" He didn't really need encouragement. So far, the man was masterful at all things sex-related. It would be hard to forget about him after he left at the end of the night.

He slid his hand between my legs, and I groaned. The crotch of my yoga pants was wet with my arousal, and since I wasn't wearing panties, it was literally soaked through. He muttered in reaction to his discovery and expertly massaged my clit through the spandex. The combination of his mouth drawing on my nipple and his hand roughly negotiating my clit sent me over the edge.

"Jesus Christ. God, Kyle, ooohhhh. Yes." I trembled through an amazing orgasm and then stilled and enjoyed the sensations moving through my torso and limbs, all the way down to my toes. I bent over him and rested my forehead on the top of his head and inhaled deeply several times. My legs felt shaky, and I was afraid I might fall if I tried to move.

"Here you go, Rocket, lie down. Let your body work its magic. Not bad, huh?" He helped me lie on the bed before scurrying to the other side to pull the covers down.

"Move over here so I can pull the covers back. I'm going to go get some water in the kitchen. Do you have bottles in the fridge?"

"Yeah, but let me do it. Not much of a hostess, am I?" I smiled lazily, endorphins making me drunk.

"You just relax. I'll be right back." He was off at a jog, and honestly, I didn't have the energy to move. He was back in the room with a couple of water bottles in no time.

"Here you go. Drink some." He had already opened the bottle when he handed it to me, so I drank a good bit before setting it on the nightstand. I rolled toward him when he climbed into bed.

"We're not done, right? Please say we're not done." I felt like a bratty kid on Christmas morning, wanting to know where the rest of the presents were after already opening a giant pile.

"Oh no, we're just getting started." He hopped back off the bed and shamelessly shucked his pants and underwear, lights still blazing brightly as if it were high noon. I sat up a little higher to really take him in.

He stopped moving and let me stare. "Well?"

"Well, what?" I chuckled.

"Everything to your liking, I presume?"

"Meh," I said in a very halfhearted tone. Although on the inside I was thinking *sweet baby Jesus in a car seat*. It had been like nine months—at least—since I'd had sex, and all of *that* was supposed to go in my unused girl parts?

Yikes.

"Meh?" he repeated. "Meh?" he said again, this time approaching the bed with a sinister look clouding his face.

Uh-oh. Maybe I'd poked the beast one too many times. Men and their toys. So sensitive.

"Take off your pants," Kyle said, his tone mimicking mine from moments ago. Now we were like two strangers talking about our commute. *Oh, it was fine. There was a fender bender on the 405. You know, same old, same old.*

I understood the game he was playing, so I lifted my ass

and pulled the yoga pants down to my calves and then kicked them free with my feet. They flew off the bed and onto the floor, somewhere near the foot of the bed.

He took ahold of my ankle and spread my leg far apart from the other, opening my already wet pussy to the cool room air. I widened my eyes at him, still surprised by his brazen approach to sex. He sat on the side of the bed near my thigh and studied my pussy for a few moments and then ran his finger down the outer edge, where I had been lasered smooth years ago.

"So sexy here. So smooth." He made the same motion again, this time with two fingers at the same time, starting at the top, spreading them wide as he moved down and meeting again at the bottom close to my opening. I could feel more wetness rushing to the spot, preparing my body for the intrusion.

If he would just indulge me...

But he seemed more interested in teasing and exploring at the moment. I sat forward, resting on my forearms, the muscles in my abdomen clenching tighter and tighter each time he neared my clit or vagina. But he skillfully avoided both, ramping me up to the point that I wanted to reach between my own legs and relieve myself.

"You're making me crazy. Please, touch me!" I moaned, letting my head fall back so I wouldn't have to look at his face while I begged.

"I've been touching you. What's the problem?" He chuckled, knowing exactly what he was doing.

"You're evil. Evil and mean and horrible," I whined.

"You don't mean that. Look how wet you are." He slid his finger over my opening, dragging the dewy moisture up and over my clit. "If I were horrible, I don't think you'd be responding this way. Do you?"

He repeated the motion a few more times before demanding an actual answer.

"Do you, Rocket?"

"No. No, I don't. God, it feels so good. Honestly, it's been so long."

"Don't you do this yourself?"

"Not the same. Not even close."

"Can I put my mouth on you here?" He swirled around my clit with his index finger, barely applying pressure so it was like a whisper, when what I really needed was a full-voiced shout.

I nodded in consent.

"Tell me, baby. Tell me what you want. It makes me hard to hear you say it." He stroked his erection in case I didn't believe what he was saying.

"Kyle? Eat my pussy. Make me come with your mouth on me." I moaned, barely able to hold back an orgasm just thinking about how good it would feel to have his lips and tongue working me over down below.

"All right, Skye." He moved onto the bed fully and settled between my thighs. "Toss me a pillow. I want to get comfortable and stay awhile." He got the pillow situated and propped at the right angle to feast on me. "Hold yourself open for me," he said, close enough to my pussy that his words fanned warm air on my wet folds.

But wait. What? Doesn't he usually do all that and I just lie here like a greedy wench and enjoy it?

"Do what you're told, Rocket, or you don't get what you

want. That simple." His words were quiet but direct. My hands flew down between my legs, and I spread my lips open so he could have full access to all the pink flesh beneath.

"Goddammit, you're so sexy." Again, I felt how close he was, and it was driving mc insane. I wanted to grab his head and mash it into my crotch and force him to go for the prize already.

"Please, for Christ's sake, Kyle, stop with the play-by-play. I'm dying. Is that what this is? Are you trying to kill me? It's working. It's honestly working." I squirmed as much as I could in front of him, needing some sort of stimulation.

Then I had the brilliant realization—my own fingers were right there. *I'll just entice him by touching myself.* I stretched my index finger toward my clit while still holding my labia back and instantly regretted the idea. Kyle sank his teeth into my finger to halt my progress.

"Okay! Okay. Never mind. Bad idea. Let go. Let. Go. Jesus." He sucked on my finger to ease the bite mark, swirling his tongue around a few times, making me forget my ire quickly. When he snaked his tongue out past my finger to touch the tip to my pussy, I nearly jolted off the bed. My nerve endings were so ramped up, the slightest touch felt like an electrical shock.

"Oh, my God, yes. Thank you. Thank you." I sighed with pleasure.

He lapped long, lazy licks up the sides of my clit before really going at the bud in the center. Over and over with the same pattern and then changing it completely when I got used to what he was doing. He pressed into my opening with the tip of his tongue and thrust in and out, making me gush with more juice for him to suck down.

"Woman, you have the sweetest pussy I think I've ever tasted. I don't know what you do different, but I don't think I'd ever get tired of this taste." His compliments came between tongue motions.

Thank God!

That was too bad, wasn't it? Since this was definitely going to be the only time his mouth would be taking that journey.

"Let go." He nudged my hands, and I released my outer lips and moved my hands away from my body altogether, using them to prop myself up a bit so I could watch him eat me. I loved the erotic sight of his mahogany hair between my thighs. I'd close my eyes and remember that exact sight in the future.

Kyle looked up across my stomach and breasts and locked eyes with me while flicking my clit with his tongue. My eyes fluttered with the pleasure as I tumbled toward climax with the added eroticism of the visual contact. His alluring cat eyes alone did crazy things to my sex, so watching them while he ate me was ten times more pleasurable.

He used his forefinger to tease around my opening, painting my slickness down to my anus and back up again. After a few repetitions, he slid his finger into me, making the first actual penetration slow and incredible.

"God, Kyle, yes. So good. That feels so good." He pushed up closer to me, tossing the pillow to the floor so nothing was between our bodies. His mouth kept a perfect rhythm on my clit while he added a second finger to the penetrating motion of the first, stretching me farther, filling me.

"So close. So close. Please don't stop." I flopped down

onto my back, twisting my fingers into his hair, needing to anchor myself to something when I came apart. The last few pumps of his hand were more aggressive, thumping into my ass with the knuckles of his fist while he buried the two fingers inside me as deeply as possible.

"Give it to me, Skye. Let me hear you, Rocket," he encouraged coarsely.

It was on me like a tidal wave. Swelling and building and then cresting and crashing. The sensation overtook me, tumbling through my torso and limbs and then crawling across my skin like the white froth of the ending breaker when it receded to the vast ocean that birthed it.

Panting, I lay grinning, completely satisfied. Kyle could pull on his pants and walk out the door, and I would be totally fine with it. But when I looked at the erection straining painfully from his body as he stood beside the bed, I knew there was no way he'd be on board with the same plan.

When did he get up? Does it even matter?

I was so blissed out, I could likely be talked into just about anything at that moment.

"Thank you. That was ridiculous. It's been a really long time since I—since a guy—well, shit...you know what I mean." I was a bumbling mess, and I could feel the heat rushing to my face with the telltale redness too, but I couldn't stop myself from babbling. "So, yeah, thanks for that." I slung my arm over my eyes, feeling like an idiot. A not-very-eloquent idiot to boot.

The bed dipped under his weight. "Scoot over." He nudged my hip with the back of his hand. When I moved about two feet, he added, "Farther, knucklehead. You're going to be right in the wet spot there. The bed's big enough for an army. Shove over." His deep chuckle warmed my heart.

Whoa, wait. Retract that completely.

There was absolutely no heart involved in anything that was happening here.

None whatsoever.

Nada.

None.

But I couldn't help admitting his concern for my comfort was sweet. If nothing else, it was thoughtful, and a lot of guys weren't even that.

I moved to the far side of the bed, and he followed me, settling somewhere in the center.

"So, what should we do about this situation?" I asked playfully, moving to take his cock into my hand before he stopped me en route.

"Well, we have a bit of a problem." He looked at me with a terrible look on his face that I couldn't read in the slightest.

"What's wrong? Did I gross you out? You don't want to do it now?" Panic crawled over me like a million little spiders, and I started to reach for the sheet to cover myself.

"Woman. Look at this." He held his dick so it stood straight up from his pelvis. Christ, he had a beautiful cock, and I licked my lips without thinking.

"Does this look like you've grossed me out or I don't want to fuck you until you can't walk?"

Well shit. When he put it like that...

"What's the problem, then?" I asked, utterly confused, looking back and forth a couple of times from his erection to his face.

"I thought I had a condom in my wallet, but I don't." His face crumbled with disappointment.

"Maybe I have one here. Let me look." I scurried off the bed and crashed to my knees on the floor and rummaged through the nightstand drawer in a fury. I knew the chances were slim to none, but I had to hold out hope. It had been a really long time since I brought a guy home. Sharing a house with Oliver kind of put the kibosh on slumber parties, and I knew I had cleaned out the drawers recently. If Oliver still lived with me it would be problem solved, but obviously that wasn't the case either.

I rested my head on the nightstand and whimpered. "How can this be happening? My virginity is going to grow back soon with this kind of luck. I was so close!"

He laughed, a real, genuine laugh, and it was a contagious sound. I crawled back onto the bed and into his outstretched arms. He kissed the top of my head and wrapped his arms around me.

An idea struck, and it was probably an irresponsible one, but I thought I'd float it and see what he thought. "How often do you get tested for STDs?"

"Oh shit, I don't know. Usually after I've had a new partner and we break up. I'm pretty religious about protection, though. I had a roommate when I first got out of college that had some crazy clap or something, and the dude was miserable. It scared the shit out of me. Ever since that, I've been neurotic about it. For a long time, I wouldn't even go down on a girl."

"Well sweet Jesus, thank God you conquered that phobia," I mumbled, but he heard every word.

"What about you? Are we going somewhere with this line of questioning or just getting to know each other better?"

"I wasn't exaggerating when I said it's been a while that I've been with a guy. Like, *a while*. And, without going into too many boring details, I have some female issues, reproductive type things, so I'm under a doctor's care regularly, and pregnancy isn't a concern." I watched his reaction, seeing if he blanched or recoiled as some men did when you brought up girly things.

When he didn't, I felt comfortable to continue. "I usually have them throw in the STD panel when I have labs done, just to be safe, you know?" Kyle nodded in understanding before I finished with my clean bill of health. "I've probably had that done twice since I've been sexually active."

He took my hand in his and interlaced our fingers. Given the amount of intimacy we'd shared already, the gesture wasn't exactly out of bounds, but still, it felt oddly sincere. I had the impulse to pull back, but he started talking and it became more awkward to withdraw.

"I'm sorry you're having issues that require a doctor's care. I know you don't want to talk about it more right now, and I get that. But if you ever need an ear, I'm a good listener."

"That's very nice of you," I said automatically because it seemed like the right thing to say at the moment.

"Well, the not-nice part of me still wants to fuck you. Really, really badly. So, if what I'm hearing us both saying is that we're both clean, you don't mind going for it without a condom, and I don't mind..." He looked down at his cock, which had already risen back to full attention at the idea.

"Okay," I said sheepishly. But again, how ridiculous to feel shy now, after that man had had his face in my crotch for the better part of the last hour?

He rolled toward me and kissed me lightly. At first, at least. I knew the beast wouldn't be far behind, and he didn't disappoint.

Moving on top of me, he nudged my legs apart with his knee and settled his weight on the bed between my thighs. The kiss grew in intensity, with Kyle stealing my breath with a combination of tongue thrusts and light nips at my lips with his front teeth. The constant mixture of sensations kept things unpredictable and exciting and added to the erotic buildup.

"God, dude," I said, panting. "I'm so glad I didn't kiss you earlier in life."

He grinned down at me, stroked hair back from my forehead, and then kissed the spot he'd just cleared. Even that felt amazing, and seriously, who'd ever been kissed on the forehead and it felt anything other than parental?

"Why's that, gorgeous girl?" He had made his way through my hair and over to my ear, tugging small sections of my tresses as he went.

"Because you would've completely ruined me for everyone else. Did you take a class or something?" I tipped my head back, wanting to give him access to any and every spot he wanted to travel. I loved having my neck kissed and sucked on more than anything.

"Thank you, I think," he said by my ear and grinded his hips into my slick pussy. "I just pay attention to what works."

"Jesus Christ. Can you fuck me, please? It feels so good

when you do that." I reached between us and took him in my hand. All movement stopped except for the slide of my grip up and down his shaft.

"That's so good." He closed his eyes, and I missed the golden glow immediately. I had gotten used to the comfort of them staring back at me all night. He pushed his arms up so he was in the position of a modified push-up, knees between my thighs, arms on either side of my shoulders, and we both watched in fascination while my powder-pink-nail-adorned fingers moved up and down.

"How's that? Tell me what to do to make it better," I said, not knowing his preferences. Some guys liked it rougher; some liked a lighter grip. As far as my experience taught me, they all liked when you toyed with and squeezed their balls, but he was too far away for me to reach.

"It's already perfect, Skye. So good. I need to be inside you, though. If that's okay?"

"Okay? Dude, I was getting ready to beg again!"

"Don't let me stop you. You know I love hearing it."

I tilted my head a little and gave his cock one last squeeze.

"Flip over. Get up on your hands and knees for me."

My absolute favorite position of all time was doggy, so I complied without a single remark. My eagerness didn't go unnoticed.

"Totally pegged you for a little puppy. I'm going to get you some furry ears and a tail. If you're really good, a spiked collar," he said, stroking himself while I settled into position in front of him.

"Don't push it," I said, looking back over my shoulder. I

wiggled my ass in invitation and added, "Now fuck me, *Papi*, and make it good."

Crack.

The sound registered before the pain, but luckily it sounded way worse than it felt. I was more shocked that he'd just slapped my rear than anything else.

"Bad puppy." He toyed with my opening a bit and ran the moisture down to my clit and made small circles over the sensitive bud and then back again. I was gearing up to make another comment encouraging him to put his dick inside me when I felt him inch forward and press the head into my vagina.

We had talked about the gap in activity for me, so I appreciated his effort to go slow, but I wanted to feel him fill me so badly, I moaned in anticipation.

"Please, Kyle, please. Do it. Fuck me."

"I'm working on it, baby. I don't want to hurt you. You'll thank me tomorrow if I go slow at first," he said, voice filled with concern.

"No, I'll thank you tomorrow if every time I take a step or sit down, I'm reminded of how well I was fucked the night before. Just do it. Please. Please, Kyle, fuck me."

"All right, Rocket. Don't say I didn't warn you, though." The edge returned to his tone, and I braced my weight onto my arms, ready for the impact.

I attempted to wiggle my ass again but didn't move very far. Kyle had his hands on my hips, holding me in place for his invasion. In the next moment, he was seated fully, smacking against my ass with his toned abdominal muscles, and the pain was so intense I was briefly blinded.

I tried to cry out, but he had anticipated my reaction and snaked his long arm forward, covering my mouth with his hand. The sound was muffled by his palm, but at least he couldn't move his hips with his body stretched over me to cover my mouth. I clawed at his hand to let him know it was safe to remove it. The initial shock of his overwhelming penetration was gone. He'd certainly tried to warn me, so there wasn't much to say in rebuke.

"Okay?" He checked in.

"Yeah." I gasped for a breath when he removed his hand. "It was more than I expected. Sorry about that."

"Hey, I don't mind screaming and yelling during sex. I actually enjoy it. I don't know what your neighbor situation is, and I don't want to be interrupted with a concerned citizen knocking on the door." He ran his palm back and forth along my spine while we spoke.

"Selfish prick," I said into the bedding.

"Guilty as charged on this one." He laughed. "Ready to move?" He pulled back marginally at first, just an inch or two to coat his length with my wetness as he went, helping the glide go nice and easy.

After about four or five thrusts, he was giving me the full length of his shaft, and I was digging my fingers into the sheets in response. Another four strokes or so, and my breath was coming in uneven chugs, the moaning that was involuntarily coming from my throat making it difficult to fill my lungs fully. The next cycle of movement, Kyle showed off a few twists of his hips that did ridiculous things to the inner walls of my pussy and lit up a light show in the backs of my eyelids. By the time he was chanting my name in time with his hip action, I knew he was close to coming, and I wasn't about to be greedy and beg him to wait for me.

It was the perfect time for the reach through to massage and squeeze his sack and send him into bliss. I took his balls in my palm and applied pressure evenly to the entire handful. It took a bit of finesse to hang to him while he continued to fuck me, but with the encouraging sounds he was making, it was worth the effort.

"Fill me up, Kyle. Do it. Let me feel it all."

"Oh, Christ! Yes! Fuck!" One last longer thrust and he stilled deep inside me. I could feel his cock jerking in my channel as he spurted his seed within me.

He slowly moved in and out a couple of times, milking out his pleasure until the very last drop was out, and then let his spent cock slide from my body. I fell forward onto my stomach and turned my face to the side on the pillow, wanting to close my eyes and fall asleep for the night.

Kyle crashed down beside me on his back, little trickles of sweat running down his temple. He'd worked hard, and hopefully, the finish was worth it all. If his orgasm was a fraction of what he had given me earlier, it was a no-brainer. It was a true shame we wouldn't be doing this again.

"My prediction was spot-on," he said, staring up at the ceiling fan above my bed. "Can we turn that on? I'm dying here."

I grabbed the remote off my nightstand and hit the button that turned the fan on. Of course, I had to hit about three different buttons before I got the right one because I never knew how the damn thing worked.

"I'll figure this thing out the day I move. I'm convinced." I laughed self-deprecatingly. "But what was this prediction you speak of, Mr. District Attorney Man?"

"Mine is the same way." He pointed to the fan. "I don't know why they don't just put one button on the thing. I'm trusted to interpret the law, but I can't turn on a ceiling fan." We both watched the blades spin round and round hypnotically, the silence of the room calming and enjoyable.

"Your prediction?" I prompted finally.

"When I called you Rocket. I was predicting you'd make me come like a rocket when I finally had the chance." His grin was wider than the Grand Canyon. "Shit, did I ever." He let his head loll to the side and stared at me. "You're an amazing woman. In case I don't have the chance to tell you that again."

"You're pretty all right yourself." I stared at the fan, avoiding the intimate moment at all costs.

"Just all right?" His voice was filled with incredulousness.

"Meh," I added to lighten the moment.

"Oh, my God. We're back to that?" He turned his entire body to the side to face me.

"You don't need your ego inflated any more than it already is. You won't get out the door, your head will be so large," I said in way of explanation.

"You'll be remembering just how large my head is tomorrow. Just like you wanted."

"This is what I'm talking about." I smacked his chest playfully with the back of my hand, and he quickly grabbed it before I could pull back.

"I like you," he said and then kissed my fingertips.

"We agreed we weren't doing this again," I reminded him, yanking my hand away.

"I'm just saying I like you. That's not a crime. Don't get all worked up. You're one of those commitment-phobic girls, huh?" he taunted while I got up and searched for my discarded clothes.

"Not necessarily. Just with you specifically," I explained as I pulled on my pants.

He twisted his face in what I guessed was a combination of confusion and insult.

"Don't get all weird on me now, Armstrong. We knew what this was going in." I tugged my shirt over my head, armor fully back in place.

"Yeah, I get it. I get it. I guess sleeping here isn't happening? Even though we're both exhausted and it would be almost dangerous for me to drive at this hour?" He turned on the puppy-dog eyes and melodrama, making me snort in laughter.

"Did you just snort? Like legit snort?" he teased.

"Well, you should see the terrible acting you're doing. It's pitiful!" I ran the brush that I kept on my nightstand through my hair.

"Did it work?" he asked hopefully.

"You know, I don't mind if you spend the night, but we both have to work in the morning," I said. "Wouldn't you rather wake up in your own house and get ready for work there? You know, get your day started in your own environment?"

"Uh, and miss the chance, however slim it may be, of

getting inside your pants again before I have to do all that? Hell no. I *am* still on the XY chromosome team."

Hmmmm. I hadn't even thought of round two.

Now I turned on the dramatic flair, acting as though I was really weighing the merits of him spending the night and having sex again. Of course, inside I had already made up my mind with a resounding *hell yes.*

"Do you snore?" I asked, as if questioning someone for a job interview.

"No. Do you?" He looked at me sideways, as if it could be a total deal breaker.

"I've never had any complaints. I'm not cooking you breakfast. I don't cook at all. You get one cup of coffee. Two if you make it yourself." Just the facts.

"Do you kick, talk, or walk in your sleep?" He followed with the next item on his mental checklist.

"No. Do you?"

"No."

"Deal." He passed. It was done. He would stay the night.

"Deal," he agreed. "Should we fuck on it?"

"Fuck on it?" There was one I hadn't heard before.

"Yeah," he said as if I were dense. "Instead of shake on it."

"Oh, my God. You're crazy." I shook my head. What a character this guy had turned out to be. It really was too bad we wouldn't be doing this again after tonight.

"Maybe. Maybe a little crazy for you." He drifted off at the end of his thought, and I didn't quite make out what he'd said.

"What did you just say?" I tried to get him to repeat himself.

"Hmm? Oh, nothing. Mind if I use the shower? I want to be fresh when you suck my dick."

"Oh. My. God." Staring at him speechless for a few beats, I finally pointed with a straight arm. "There." I motioned toward my bathroom. "You can use the towels that are hanging in there. They're clean, and there's a washcloth too. If I'm sleeping when you come out? Don't wake me."

I climbed back into bed as he got out and went into the bathroom. Sleep claimed me minutes after my head hit the pillow. Even though he didn't wake me when he came out of the shower, we did have a second round sometime during the night and then a third when we woke up in the morning.

Still, when he drove off that morning, I swore I would never have him back at my place again. But something about that left a hollow pit in the bottom of my stomach.

Except my stomach must have moved up higher overnight and lodged in the middle of my chest, because the place I was feeling pain was in the area where my heart used to be.

CHAPTER SIX

"Hey, sunshine. How are you this morning?" I called Laura on my way to work. I still wasn't sure I'd share about Kyle, but I wanted to check in on my favorite Easy Bake Oven.

"Not so great. Morning sickness has kicked in, and I can barely get away from the toilet long enough to take a shower," she said. "I considered barfing while I was in there but figured cleaning out the drain would make me barf again. Oh, God"— she let out a pitiful moan—"I shouldn't have said that."

"Oh, honey, I'll let you go. Maybe some flat ginger ale? Isn't that a thing?" I offered in sympathy.

"No, it'll pass. I don't want to hang up. Dwelling on it definitely makes it worse." She put on her brave voice. I'd recognize it anywhere from our days at UCLA. She went through a lot of family drama when her parents split up after twenty-some years of marriage, but she'd soldiered on through it all.

"You poor thing. I hope this doesn't last too long. I think I've heard people say just the first couple of weeks, right?"

"I'm not sure. I just downloaded a book," she said, sounding glum. "Guess I have something new to listen to on my commute. The couple in my romance novel will have to keep the home fires burning while I figure out how to settle my stomach."

"Spoiler alert. They live happily ever after," I told her in a deadpan voice.

"They always do, Skye. They always do," she answered, matching my tone.

"How do you keep reading those? One after the other? I don't get it. So not like real life. At all."

"Maybe that's the point? Have you ever thought of that? Just escaping for a little while?" Laura offered it to me as something to think about.

"I guess it makes more sense to look at it that way." I shrugged, even though she couldn't see me.

"You seem even more jaded this morning than usual," she said suspiciously. "What's got the bee in your bonnet?" Leave it to one of my closest friends to call me on my shit.

I tried to sound casual as I answered. "No bee."

"I can hear the buzzing from here, girlfriend."

"Nah. I'm good." The second attempt at casual might drive it home.

"Okay, whatever you say. So, did you file your paperwork or whatever you were texting me about yesterday afternoon?" Wisely, she changed the subject.

"I did. And you're never going to guess who's running for the same effing position." And we ended up right back on the subject I was trying to avoid. "I mean, of all the goddamn city council districts, he lives in mine. It's so unbelievable, it has to be true."

"Noooo. That guy from Itza's? What was his name? Kevin? No, Kyle. Yeah...Kyle Armstrong."

I couldn't believe she guessed on the first try. "That's the very one."

"Wow, that's some coincidence."

"Yeah." I sighed quietly, remembering that night. That kiss in the street. The kissing last night. The *everything* last night.

"Hey, are you there? Did I lose you? Skye? Are you going through the canyon? Skye?"

"No, I'm here. Sorry," I answered when I finally pulled my head back into the present.

"Oh, thought I lost you. Why did you get so quiet?" Like a dog with a bone, she'd keep on it until I answered.

"I don't know. No reason."

"Goddamnit. You're so full of shit. What aren't you telling me? That's the second time you've lied this morning. You're the worst liar, by the way." At least she was staying good-natured about it. So far.

"I know, I know," I whined. I didn't even know where to begin. I still wasn't sure I wanted to tell her. She was my best girlfriend, and I didn't know if I wanted to say it all out loud. Because that would make it all too real.

"Ooooohh, hell!"

"What? What happened? Are you okay? Is it the baby?" I was playing dumb, and we both knew it.

"Don't give me that bullshit," she said in a very serious tone.

"What?" I tried the innocent bit again.

"You fucked him."

"What? Who?" I tried to sound confused and knew it was a long shot.

"Skye. Blue. Delaney. You stop it right now." Laura was

getting tired of the runaround. I could hear it in her voice, and when she went for the full-name usage, playtime was over.

"Oh no you didn't with the whole proper name."

"I did. And you fucking spill your guts right now."

My last hope was motherhood guilt. "Need I remind you, you are with child? That mouth of yours is going to rub off on that innocent fetus." If that didn't work, I'd be singing like a canary.

"Stop trying to change the subject," she said impatiently.

"Uh-oh." I made a bunch of static noises with my mouth. "I'm going through the canyon for real now. You're breaking up." Static noises. "Laura? Laura, can you hear me?"

"Just stop," she said, utterly bored.

"Okay, I fucked him. It was amazing. We fucked in the middle of the night and again this morning before he left my place, and it was ridiculous those times too. Happy?" I shot, as if she were the one who needed to defend herself.

"Does he have a big dick?" Laura asked without hesitation.

"Enormous. And he knows how to use it. Like, really knows how to use it, Laura. It makes me want to break out in tears just thinking about it." My voice shifted into a full whimper by the end of the sentence.

"Tears of happiness, I presume? That you finally found someone who knows what the hell they're doing after the string of losers you've been putting up with?" Laura, on the other hand, sounded like she was bouncing up and down in her seat with excitement.

"No. Tears of sorrow." I hated to burst her bubble, but it was the cold, hard truth.

"I'm not following. I think this baby is already eating away at my brain." Her confusion was actually adorable at the moment, for whatever reason, but I needed her to understand so she wouldn't badger me about trying to make it work with Kyle.

"Because I'm never sleeping with him again. How the hell can I? He's my opponent in a freaking election."

"So what?" she fired back immediately.

"So what? *So what?* Do you know the field day the press and public would have with information like that?" I thought about it for all of two seconds before continuing. "Oh, my God. Just thinking about it makes me want to crawl under a rock for how fucking stupid I was. It would be career suicide, Laura. No one would ever take me seriously again in the political arena. Ever. Ugh. Talk about sudden death."

"I think you're being a little overdramatic." Laura's classic ability to trivialize things rubbed me raw.

"Are you kidding me? The fastest way for a woman to lose credibility in any field these days? Have sex with someone in the same job pool. Even in a remotely related one." It was exasperating that she didn't see what I was talking about.

"Well, your secret dies with me, you know that. You've told me other things over the years that I haven't breathed a word of to anyone," she said solemnly.

"I know. I know," I answered, calming down. "I love you so much for that."

"How good was it? I need details." Her switch back to the lighter part of the topic was so appreciated. It felt so good to girl talk with her.

"You're such a dog," I teased.

"You know it, and now that I have a baby on board, there will be zero action in this camp for at least a year. I had to sign a damn contract swearing to it!"

That little detail may have been a slip, but I couldn't help commenting about it.

"Seriously? It's your sister, for Christ's sake. Couldn't she just take your word for it?"

"Hello? You've met my sister, right?" she said.

"Point made."

"Plus, her husband is more uptight than she is. It's no wonder they couldn't make a baby on their own. Jesus. Can you imagine those two fucking?"

"Oh, don't do that to my imagination, Laura. Some things you can't unsee."

"Right?" Laura laughed stiffly. "But let's circle back to you and Mr. Cat Eyes. Are those contacts?"

"No. Not that I could tell, anyway. I mean, they were still there in the middle of the night."

We both burst out laughing like we used to when we were up all night studying in college, so tired we were punch-drunk.

"He's a kinky motherfucker, isn't he?" she asked in a whisper.

"Mmmm, I don't know if I'd call it kinky. Definitely dominant, which, you know me, right up my alley," I whispered in answer. "Why are we whispering?" We both laughed until I was wiping tears off my cheeks.

"God, you're such a bitch right now. So jealous," she finally said when the laughter died down.

"Hey, don't be a hater. You know I've put in my time lately," I said, reminding her of my recent bad run of men.

"True. True. That last dude, oh my God, what was his name? Landis? Who the fuck names their child Landis?"

"Try screaming that out in the middle of sex! So awkward. Not that there was ever anything to be screaming about with Mr. Micropenis. I thought that was a made-up condition. Yeah. No."

Laura laughed again, but we had to say goodbye soon after because I was close to work. I promised I'd check in with her later and see how she was feeling.

I pulled into the parking structure and found a spot rather quickly—a strange occurrence for prime working hours—and I did a quick mental check. Nope, definitely not a state holiday, so I chalked it up to luck. A girl was due once in a while, right?

When I got to my desk, I had a ton of emails to deal with and needed to check in with Bailey. Since I'd spent my entire commute bullshitting with Laura, I hadn't had a chance to talk with her like I had hoped. I needed to be better at managing my time for the rest of the day, or I'd never get everything done on the to-do list she'd emailed me the night before.

Of course, that was before the epic booty call that had erased every responsible thing from my mind for the following twelve hours.

I needed to find a way to absolve myself from the guilt steadily eating a hole through the lining of my stomach. It was either guilt or the jet fuel Kyle had made me as a substitute for coffee before he left.

Saying goodbye had been a little harder than I'd expected.

Something about knowing I'd be seeing him on the campaign trail over the coming weeks and thinking about his expert mouth—and dick—every time I did made my routine cut-and-run more difficult than I was used to.

My boss of the moment, Jack Carter, poked his head into my shared office around midmorning and asked me to come down to his office when I had a few minutes. Odd, considering an email or phone call would've done the same task without attracting all the attention of everyone else in the pen. I waited about ten minutes, then headed over to see what he needed.

I knocked on his outer door when his assistant wasn't at his desk.

"Yeah!" he called from inside.

"It's Skye," I answered back, loud enough for him to hear through the closed door.

"Hey, come in. I was hoping it was you," he said, opening the door and inviting me into his office.

I walked in but didn't close the door behind me. I was never super comfortable being behind a closed door with a man, even in a professional setting.

"Hi. You wanted to see me?"

"I did. Do you mind if I close this?" he asked and reached for the door.

Keeping direct eye contact with him, I said, "I'd be more comfortable leaving it open, unless you need to say something confidential. I think your assistant is on a break, so we shouldn't be overheard by anyone." I planted a neutral smile on my face and waited for Jack to continue.

"Between you and me, the guy is all but useless." He went

around and sat at his desk and began shuffling papers. "I don't know how these kids even get through college. My apologies if I made you uncomfortable by wanting to close the door, though." He looked up from his paperwork for the first time. "Please sit." He motioned to the leather chair on the opposite side of his desk.

After sitting, I explained, "I had an unfortunate experience where some ambitious coworkers made up rumors that my supervisor and I were doing inappropriate things behind his closed office door. So now I try to avoid that sort of dumpster fire if I can help it."

"Makes perfect sense," he said, shaking his head in disbelief. "I'll get right to the point. I'm sure you have a lot going on now that you're campaigning." An unspoken bond was tied between us. We were both embarking on campaigns in a very volatile political climate in a city that was just rocked by scandal. Together, we could try to restore peoples' faith in their elected politicians.

"Congratulations." He finally looked up from twisting his wedding ring. "It's a historical time for our city."

"Thank you. I'm excited and scared to death. But I'm ready for whatever comes my way. I've been gearing up for this for years. It's the next logical step."

"Can't say I blame you, Skye. Especially with everything that's happened around here in the past few months. What does surprise me, however, is that you didn't stick it out and seek appointment in the city manager's office. That's where you've been focusing all your talent for years." He leveled his stare directly at me, and I felt like a spotlight could flip on at any moment.

"True. Very true," I countered. "But the mayoral race is going to be very unpredictable. The citizens have lost a lot of faith in this office as a whole. I can't count on whoever wins knowing that I'm the right person for the job if they've never worked with me before. Then where does that leave me?"

"You're not confident I'll win?" he said, leaning forward in his chair, propping his elbows on his desk.

"That's not what I'm saying. Not at all. I just have to focus on a more solid plan for myself. Too many unknowns in the city manager spot right now. Plus, with the city council seat, I get the experience of being on a campaign trail and not just relying on an appointment." If this were an interview, I was nailing these answers.

"You're a bright woman, Skye. No matter where you land, you're going to succeed." He lowered his voice, making a visible nod to the open door. "You're head and shoulders above the rest of your peers here. If your opponents in the city council race are any of these buffoons, you're a shoo-in. You can count on my endorsement. If you want it, that is."

"Wow. Jack, that's really great," I said, touched by his faith in me. "I can't thank you enough." I stood and thrust my hand toward him to shake in gratitude. I couldn't wait to get back to my computer to email Bailey. She would love the tidbit for my announcement press release.

The temporary mayor walked me to the entry of his office, where his assistant was just coming to knock on the doorjamb.

"Oh, sorry, Jack. I didn't realize you had an appointment. Hi, Ms. Delaney. Wait, were you on the schedule? I don't remember seeing your name."

"It was impromptu, Norman. Relax, son," said Jack, sounding affable. "It happens. I went by Skye's office and asked her to drop by when she had a minute. You weren't at your desk when she came by. Which, by the way, you need to tell me when you take a break. We've discussed this before." Great. Jack was dressing down his helper right in front of me.

Awkward.

"Sorry, sir. Won't happen again," the nebbish guy replied, adjusting his glasses. "Your actual ten forty-five is here." He motioned toward the person waiting in the sitting area of the office.

Motherfucker.

"Kyle! Come on in. Do you know Ms. Delaney? She's in the city manager's office."

"No, I don't believe we've met. Pleasure." He stretched his hand toward me, and I had the strongest urge to smack it away and kick him in the balls. What was he doing sniffing around Jack's office? Probably looking for the endorsement I just got.

"Are you sure we haven't met before?" I said, looking quizzically at him, as if trying to place his face. "You look familiar. Are you in maintenance?" He was dressed super casually, and I made every effort to point that out, subtly, of course.

He barked out a laugh, his gorgeous golden eyes glowing while he shook my hand, holding on about three seconds too long.

I pulled my hand away and turned to the acting mayor. "Jack, I'll have my campaign manager contact you for a quote, okay?"

"Sure, Skye. Anything you need," he answered, unaware of how perfectly he just played his part in my setup.

I looked at Kyle one last time before turning to leave. "Nice to meet you." I was so glad I'd worn my best-fitting pencil skirt so he could watch my ass sway as I took a mini victory walk out of the mayor's office while he stood there trying to process what had just happened.

This race was *on*. And the best woman was definitely going to win.

♦ ♦ ♦ ♦

At lunch, I left my office and went to the little café around the corner. Bailey met me there so we could go over some critical plans she said couldn't wait until later. I had just sat down at the little bistro table when the chimes above the door jingled, catching my attention. She had been prattling on and on about an engagement that absolutely had to be attended, and I had tuned out completely when I locked stares with...who else?

Kyle.

Was he following me?

Of course, the café was a block from our office and also a very common spot for city employees to have lunch. When I did a quick scan of the place, there were at least four other tables hosting people I recognized.

He did his business at the counter and then made a beeline for our table.

"Can I talk to you for a minute?" he asked quietly.

"No, you may not. I'm very busy at the moment," I answered without looking up to him.

"It'll just take a minute." He stared at me, clearly with no intention of leaving without talking to me first.

"Excuse me. This will take less than a minute," I said to Bailey, and then I stormed out the front door. This time the chime above the door sounded like a siren belting instead of a pleasant lullaby.

"Dude. Why? I'm having a business meeting in there. So embarrassing." I swung my whole body toward him, and he ducked back like I might hit him.

"And what you pulled in Carter's office wasn't?"

"You had that coming."

"How do you figure?"

I tilted my head to the side. "Clearly you were trying to do an end run for his endorsement."

"An end run? How so? I don't have to run my campaign strategy by you first." He shook his head in disbelief.

I just stammered. Because he was right. *Fuck*. He didn't owe me any type of explanation. Or consideration. At all.

"I'm sorry." I hated those words more than any others, but I had to say them. "I was out of line. It was immature of me to act that way. Although I didn't really do anything, per se. Except maybe add a little sway to the moneymaker when I walked away." I thumbed over my shoulder and tried for a sheepish grin.

"Yeah, thanks to that sway, I had to sit and talk to the mayor with a fucking hard-on for twenty minutes. Pretty sure he was in the same fucking boat." His eyes regained their spark as he spoke, and I knew we were back in peaceful territory.

"Ewwww." I shuddered for extra effect.

He cocked his head to the side. "XY chromosome."

I heaved in a breath.

"You owe me for that stunt," he said matter-of-factly.

"You're insane," I fired back in the same emotionless tone.

"I'm coming over tonight."

"No. You. Are. Not."

"Eight o'clock. Keep the door unlocked." We locked eyes, daring one another to chicken out.

"No. Kyle, I'm serious. No. We agreed." I had to keep my head on straight.

He shrugged as if it were all so simple. "Well, you fucked that up today. Now you owe me."

"I have an engagement tonight. I won't be home until ten."

"Fine. I'll be there at ten o'clock, then."

I huffed again and started to come up with another reason why he couldn't come over, but he headed me off at the pass.

"This will be a lesson to you," he told me, staring me down. I could feel my heart hammering in my chest.

"Pardon?" I asked incredulously, although my voice cracked on the delivery.

"A *lesson*. To fight fair from this point forward. Otherwise, booty-call penance. I think it's a very reasonable and equitable deal. If you're being honest with yourself at least." The sexy-grin punctuation was the panty slayer.

"If I'm being honest with myself?" I asked, voice dripping with incredulity.

He closed the final few inches and spoke right beside my ear, his voice so low and gravelly, I thought I might have heard my clit whimper. "Are you going to fight me so soon after the last time? You think you'd learn. Maybe you're looking for punishments?"

Standing up straight, I said, "You're really too full of yourself, Armstrong. It's going to get you in trouble if you're not careful."

"I'll tell you what. I'll worry about me. You worry about you. Deal?" His voice went back to its conversational tone. Anyone overhearing our conversation would think nothing of it.

"I'm not making any deals with you. At all." I turned abruptly to head back to Bailey, who looked very frustrated with having to wait while we had our little chat out of her earshot.

"Oh, Rocket?" he called after me just as I reached for the door handle to go back inside.

I swung my head back toward him, hoping to God no one had heard him use that nickname. *What?* I mouthed.

He held up ten fingers to remind me of the time he would be stopping by that evening. I rolled my eyes dramatically and turned back to go inside. I was kicking myself for not being more forceful when telling him no. But I also knew the truth.

I couldn't wait to be horizontal with the motherfucker again.

When I sat down across from Bailey, she started right in with the twenty questions. "Isn't that Kyle Armstrong? One of the other candidates running against you?"

"The very same." I took an abnormally large bite of the sandwich I'd ordered.

"You seem tense. Is he harassing you? We can have a

restraining order filed against him. We can use it against him in the campaign too. It would be awful for his public image." Her eyes lit up like she would enjoy nothing more.

"He's harmless," I said, finally chewing all the food in my mouth.

"How well do you know him?"

"Not really well at all." I took another enormous bite, hoping she would stop with the questions about Kyle.

"Skye?" Her tone was one of warning.

"Hmmph?" Food-filled mouth replies weren't coherent after all.

"This is probably a good time to outline a few ground rules we need to have if we're going to work together." She moved her untouched salad to the side and leaned forward.

I widened my eyes, trying to seem surprised at her directness, even though I wasn't surprised at all.

"Not too many rules but a few key things I just can't budge on. Okay?"

I wiped my mouth with the paper napkin on my tray. "Ooookkkaaay."

"I need you to be honest with me. On all things," she said. "If I ask you something, you need to tell me the truth. I'm not here to judge you or become invested in your personal life. I can't be caught off guard or find out details that I should've already known from the press or social media. That makes sense, right?" She looked at me over the rim of her glass as she took a sip of her iced tea.

"One hundred percent," I said, and I meant it. "I'm a pretty honest person all around, Bailey. Oliver can vouch for that. It's not always the most popular personality trait, trust me. But I've always said, the truth never changes, so you're safer sticking with it from the start."

"That's a great motto to have, Skye," she said. "Especially in the political world. It will get harder and harder to live by as you move up through the ranks, I'm afraid."

"I'll do my best," I said.

"So how well do you know Kyle Armstrong?" She leveled her stare directly at me, and it was more uncomfortable than anything my mother ever brought to the table. The fact that I had just lied to her and then purported to be a truth-loving citizen was too embarrassing for words.

"I slept with him last night." In for a penny, in for a pound, right? No sense sugarcoating the situation.

"Thank you," she said. "Please don't lie to me again. I seriously don't care who you sleep with. I do have to caution you, however, if it's going to be him, that you are beyond discreet or you're going to lose major credibility with voters. And *you* will, not him."

"Why would it affect me and not him? We're running in the same race." Even though I had my own theory, I wanted to hear Bailey's seasoned opinion back it up.

"The world isn't truly equal, Skye. I know you're still young and idealistic, but you've had to have noticed that, at least on some level, by now."

"Of course, I have. Though usually when I voice my theory, people tell me I'm just being paranoid, or archaic, that the times have changed and men and women in the workplace have progressed passed certain stigmas."

Bailey looked at me sideways before continuing. "You and I both know the truth, and honestly, I'm not sure some things will ever change. A man sleeps with a woman, or many women even, and he's a stud. A hero, maybe, to some. Turn the tables and publicize a woman sleeping around, and what does that make her?" She waited for my response.

"A slut," I supplied.

"Exactly. Or an opportunist, or a no-talent sleeping her way to the top. You name it, there are a hundred different ways to cast the stone. Trust me, if that news gets out? You're the one taking the hit, not him." She picked up her tea again but didn't drink.

"I'm with you on this one, Bailey, one hundred percent."

"Again, I'm not saying you can't have a relationship with the guy. Or any other guy. I'm just saying you need to be very careful right now," she cautioned. "You are living under a microscope. You may think something seems harmless, but I have seen the press make mountains out of molehills and destroy people's careers, Skye. I'd hate to see that happen to you over a piece of ass."

Just when she sat back in her chair and relaxed a bit, her cell phone vibrated on the table. As she looked at it, I watched her face go from concerned campaign manager to giggly girlfriend in seconds. It helped keep her in perspective for me. She was still human underneath all her professional veneer, and at the end of the day, she was the woman Oliver was head over heels in love with.

"One guess who that's from," I teased.

"That apparent, huh? I think my game face has completely

lost all hope." She playfully slumped down in her chair in defeat.

"Luckily it's just me sitting here." I winked conspiratorially. "Secret's safe with me."

"So back to business," she said, sitting up tall again. "I want to run through what you can expect at the dinner tonight. The event is put on by the Rotary Club as a meet-and-greet for the city council candidates. I have you sitting at a table with two members from the water district and their wives, and I'm hoping the school board is sending a representative as well. All of the people at your table will be from your district, of course." Her professional demeanor slid back into place like a well-worn suit.

"Thank you for arranging all of that," I said, pushing the rest of my lunch away for the waitress to clear.

"Skye, that's my job."

"That doesn't mean I don't appreciate you."

"Well, you're welcome. But I want to really hammer out your platform between now and the time you leave for this thing. So, is there any way you can take the rest of the afternoon off? And where are you with the time-off request?" She took one last drink of her tea before the girl cleared our table.

"Oh! That reminds me. I forgot to tell you since we were interrupted when we first sat down and got off on *that* tangent," I said, slapping my head. "Carter said he's officially endorsing me. He'll give you a quote for a press release if you reach out to him." I was bouncing in my seat by the time I finished telling her because it was really a coup to have his backing.

"Wow! Skye, that's amazing. How did that come about?

What did you say to get him to agree to that?" she asked, stuffing her phone into her bag.

"Nothing really. He called me into his office this morning and basically asked me why I wasn't sticking around for city manager, and I told him—you know—pretty much everything we've discussed, and he said it all made sense. He said he thought I was smart and great for the job and head and shoulders above my peers." I couldn't help but toot my own horn to Bailey so she knew other people saw my worth.

"So awesome," she said. "Good for you. I'll definitely be contacting him." She made notes on her iPad while we talked and then shoved it into her briefcase.

"Armstrong wasn't so happy with the news," I added in the interest of full disclosure.

"What made you tell him?" We both stood and started toward the door.

"He asked. He was waiting to see Carter when I came out of his office, and Carter said something about having you contact him for a quote, right in front of Kyle. He put two and two together. That's what that little conversation was about." I motioned toward the front door of the café where Kyle and I had talked before.

"Well, he was probably meeting Carter for the exact same reason. You just beat him to the punch," said Bailey.

"When I told him Carter called me in, not the other way around, it just added insult to injury. I may have enjoyed that part a little bit." I grinned widely at the information.

"Try your very best to be a good sport," Bailey advised. "Sometimes it's hard. I understand that. Especially in a fast, small race like this. There are only a few big endorsements to get and three candidates. So the competition is cut-throat. But being gracious and graceful at winning *and* losing is key." As hard as they were to keep swallowing, Bailey's tips were helpful.

"Thank you for that advice. I will definitely be playing that on repeat. Some of this stuff doesn't come as second nature in a competitive situation. You do realize that, right? It feels more natural to win at all costs, you know?" We stood out front of the café chatting.

"Of course I do. That's why I will continue to remind you of them." She smiled sweetly and then laughed. "You're going to be great. And we're going to be a great team, you and me."

"I think so too. Let me go back to the office and see if I can bug out for the rest of the afternoon. I'll call you on my way home, whenever that is. Hopefully sooner rather than later. Is Carter going to this dinner tonight?" I asked before we parted company.

"He shouldn't be. It's mainly for city councils that have seats open in LA and Ventura counties. He wasn't on the guest list when I looked last, but sometimes they add the bigger guests' names at the end when they clear other commitments, so he may show up at the last minute."

"All right. I'll call you. Thanks for meeting me."

"Again...my job," she said, preparing to leave.

"I know, I know."

We hugged quickly, and I dashed back to my office to wrap up anything that couldn't wait until the next day. I stayed clear of Tara and my other coworkers and kept my nose buried in my work. I left for home to get ready for the dinner about an hour later when everyone else went to the break room for their afternoon respite. They probably didn't even notice I was gone. At least that was my hope.

The best news waited for me in my email inbox. My time-off request was approved, so as of the following day, I had two weeks off to focus on my campaign.

While Kyle Armstrong was stuck behind his desk all day, doing work for the district attorney, I'd be beating the campaign trail like a maniac, making damn sure the best candidate won this race.

Victory—thy name is Skye Delaney!

CHAPTER SEVEN

"My hope, if elected, is to develop a few of the vacant lots in the Shadow Hills neighborhood and create family-friendly parks where parents can take their children to play. Have you been to Pershing Square in the heart of downtown? Something like that would be ideal," I explained to the small group that gathered around as I spoke.

I'd taken the ideas I'd shared with Laura and fine-tuned them into a feasible campaign agenda and hit the ground running, being sure to hit those key points any and every chance I got.

Young families were fleeing our city for the Inland Empire and other outlying suburbs in droves. They were hoping to raise their children in neighborhoods where their little ones could play on greenbelts, climb on jungle gyms, and walk safely around their communities. LA had that at one time; there was no reason we couldn't have it again.

Reporters asked questions about my plans, and the more I talked, the more passionate I became. Kyle watched from the edge of the crowd, a seemingly proud smile on his handsome face. As the crowd dispersed, some reporters straggled behind to get quotes and pictures, which I happily posed for.

The dinner was a complete success. In addition to the

media coverage, I was able to hobnob with a lot of key players in my district and really get out and grip and grin with a lot of my constituents.

Bailey had asked me questions in preparation to solidify my opinion on issues facing my district, and that was a godsend. A lot of the same topics came up while I talked to the community members, and I was thankful I was able to answer their questions with confidence. Working at city hall for so many years also served me well.

To my surprise, Kyle did very little to interact with the media at the event. He was breathtaking in a perfectly fitting, navy-blue, pinstriped suit, very crisp white shirt, and gold-patterned tie, which brought out his magical eyes. I did my very best to be professional with him the entire evening. The few pictures he did pose for included me and Lloyd Jessup, the third candidate.

"Did you two match your outfits on purpose?" joked a young reporter. His photographer snapped pictures while he asked us a few questions.

Kyle and I looked at each other and then smiled at the photographer graciously, just like we were taught to do.

"Oh, look at that, Mr. Armstrong. We do match. That is a very handsome suit you're wearing."

"Thank you, Ms. Delaney. Quite the compliment coming from such a beautiful woman as yourself."

The journalist watched our exchange with keen eyes, but the photographer quickly lost interest and moved on to another picture opportunity at another grouping of people, dragging him along. He looked back over his shoulder a few times as he walked away, making me feel uncomfortable. It was probably my own paranoia getting the best of me, but something felt off with the guy.

Lloyd moved away the moment the picture was snapped, leaving us standing alone. Kyle moved to stand behind me. Anyone watching would think nothing of our interaction. He was a normal distance away.

"Don't drink too much, Rocket. I can't have you falling asleep on me," he said, looking in another direction completely.

"You need to shut your mouth when we're in public," I said, my lips barely moving. "No option on that. Did you get a strange vibe from that last reporter?" I busied myself with the hemline of my dress.

"Don't be such a worrywart. He's just doing his job," he said. "No one's paying any attention to us. Look around. They're all so busy kissing Carter's ass, they don't even know if we're still in the building or not." He took a long drink from the glass of water he was holding.

"That's not a bad idea, actually. Leaving. My feet are killing me." I sighed.

"I give a killer foot massage."

"Why am I not surprised?"

"Leave now." His voice dropped into that dangerous, commanding zone I couldn't be rational about. "I'll be fifteen minutes behind you. I'll meet you in the tub. I like lots of bubbles."

"You're insane," I responded, tossing my empty water bottle into the recycling bin.

"Maybe. But you're thinking about it."

I didn't have a comeback. All I could think about was a foot massage. And now a hot, luxurious bubble bath too.

"Go. You're just wasting time standing there having that internal argument with yourself," he said just before the teachers' union representative, Marcie Merkel, came up to say good night to him. I noticed she'd been keeping visual tabs on him most of the night.

When she was gone, I said, "I'm really starting to hate you."

"I think it's quite the opposite."

Again, no comeback. At all.

Because again, he isn't wrong.

I walked away without saying another word to the bastard. I made a fairly quick lap around the room, shaking hands and thanking people for coming out and letting people know where they could find more information about my campaign. All the usual niceties I'd heard candidates say a million times. Finally, it was my turn to be the one giving the spiel, and I was in my element.

When I got back to my place, I headed straight to my bathroom and started running the water for the tub. I added a generous amount of bubble bath to the water and ducked into my closet to hang up my dress and put away my jewelry. My hair was already styled in an updo for the evening, so I left it that way so it wouldn't get wet in the tub. Before climbing in, I quickly put on my robe and went back out to the living room to unlock the front door.

Like before, I left the front light off to ensure no one could see Kyle coming in at the late hour. Hopefully that actually worked and I wasn't just telling myself it would for peace of mind. The reporter's face from earlier came to mind with crystal clarity. I shook my head a bit to rid myself of the paranoid thought and went back to the bathroom.

I put some relaxing music on my phone and left it on the bathroom counter and then turned out most of the lights in the room, dropped my robe on the ledge by the tub, and slithered into the water. I groaned the minute my sore feet were fully submerged. I'd had no idea just how badly they were hurting until they were underwater and being soothed by the heat.

Only a few minutes passed before I heard the front door open and then quietly shut. Hopefully he'd remembered to flip the lock into place too. By the time he got to the bathroom, his suit coat was off and he was pulling his tie from the collar of his shirt. We didn't say anything to each other. I watched him strip, button by button and then the zipper, until he stood naked by the side of the tub.

"Did you lock the front door?"

He just nodded, and honestly, I kind of liked the silent Kyle. No ego to deal with, no smart remarks. Just gorgeous face, alluring eyes, and sexy-as-sin body to take in.

"Come on in. I think I remember a promise of a foot rub?" I pointed my toe out of the water, and he grinned, stepping into the tub on the opposite end from where I sat. When he settled in, he leaned his head back on the edge of the tub.

"God this feels good after a long day, doesn't it?" He sighed.

"Mmmm hmmm." I was in the exact same pose as he was on my end, thinking I could fall asleep in a few minutes if left undisturbed.

It didn't take long for him to find my body beneath the suds, though. He grabbed my calf and placed it in his lap so my foot was in the perfect position for him to rub.

Oh, God. His strong thumb pressed from my heel to the ball of my foot in one long stroke, and I swore I saw angels.

"How did you know that was exactly where it hurt?"

"Baby, I see the shoes you wear. That can't feel good after an entire day." He made the thumb movement again, and the bliss was even better the second time.

"Sweet Jesus. Honest to God, so good," I purred. "I will pay you to come to do this every single day."

"In blow jobs? Deal." He chuckled but likely wasn't joking.

"You should not talk. It ruins things," I said without opening my eyes.

He squeezed my big toe flat between his thumb and index finger, and while he may have wanted it to be some sort of punishment for being bratty, it too was heavenly.

Kyle continued mashing each toe, one by one, between his fingers, until he got to the little baby on the end and made his way back again. Then he moved down to the next joint, where my toes joined with my foot, and did it there too.

I moaned and praised his massaging prowess as he went, hoping he would never stop. He changed to the other foot, and it was equally amazing. By the time each foot had equal attention, the water was cooling off.

"Do you have towels nearby that we can use?" he asked quietly.

"Nope. Drip drying for you." I grinned with my eyes closed. There was something irresistible about teasing him, even when answering the simplest of questions.

He stood up first, sloshing water over my body. The last of the bubbles splashed into my face.

"Oh, sorry, did I do that? My bad." His voice didn't hold an ounce of remorse, but I had definitely deserved his playful retaliation, so I just wiped my face with my fingers while grinning.

"Up you go." He held his hand out to steady me while I stood.

I grabbed a towel from the towel bar and wrapped myself up. "Thank you," I said softly, looking up at him. "And thank you for the amazing foot rub. That was the best ever. Can you move in with me?"

"Don't tease. I'll have my bags packed by morning." He leaned down and kissed me before I could respond to what he'd just said. Of course I was joking when I made the offer, but I wasn't so sure he was when he replied.

I was swept away by the kiss. Any worrisome thoughts were erased by his magical mouth and wicked tongue. With a sharp tug, Kyle pulled me against his body by wrapping his strong arms around my shoulders. He caged me helplessly by pinning my arms to my sides while he ministered to me. I itched to touch him too, but I was confined by his muscular biceps, and the helpless feeling was so delightful. I gave in to it like a rag doll.

"That's it. Just let me," he said against my lips when he felt my body relax.

I opened my eyes and lips simultaneously to say something in retort, but he filled my mouth with his tongue, taking away the possibility. After I relaxed again, he moved across my jaw with small kisses and nibbles until he got to my ear. He licked around the shell several times until every inch of my exposed skin had goose bumps.

"Are you cold? Let's get under the covers." He leaned back to look at me.

"It's from you," I said, narrowing my eyes. "Not the temperature. My ears and neck are very sensitive. And you're damn well aware of it. You just want to hear me say it to boost your overinflated ego."

"Maybe." He laughed. "But let's get into bed so I can have my way with you." He waggled his eyebrows, and I giggled.

"Hmm. Okay!" Really, what was a girl going to say to that? No?

Kyle took my hand and led the way into my room. We each went to a different side of the bed and worked together to put the decorative pillows on the chair and dresser and pull the covers down.

I got on the bed, and Kyle walked back into the bathroom and came back with his clothing. He laid everything on top of the pillows on the chair and pulled the tie from the pile.

"Can I use this?" He held up his tie, taut between his two fists.

I sat up a little higher. "What did you have in mind?" I was no stranger to bedroom games—in fact, I preferred them. I didn't need the whole protocol thing, with the "Sir" and a cage under the bed to sleep in, but vanilla sex wasn't my jam, and I knew from our previous conversation that it wasn't his either.

"Can I just see where the moment takes me?" he asked,

prowling toward the bed.

"No gags. No visible marks. No anal. Other than that, I think we should be fine," I replied.

"Well, that's all the good stuff," he said, shoulders slumping and pretending to whine. But the mischievous look on his face said he was playing.

"Do you ever bottom?" I asked curiously.

"No."

"Are you open to trying?"

"No."

"Why so closed off about it?" I pressed.

"I can't imagine that working out for me. At all." He shrugged.

"You never know. You might be surprised."

"What I'm not surprised about is that you switch. I can totally see you topping someone. Makes me hard thinking about it, actually." He grabbed his cock, tie still wrapped around his fist.

"News flash, chief, you were hard when you got here an hour ago." I wouldn't be able to pull my eyes away from his groin even if a little car full of clowns pulled up and parked in my bedroom and twenty-seven face-painted entertainers hopped out and did magic tricks.

"I've been hard since Carter's office this morning," he said. "Even beating off didn't make it go away. You're like an illness I can't seem to shake." He climbed onto the bed with one knee.

"Like herpes?" I finally looked up at his face again and grinned.

"Are you sure I can't use this as a gag?" he asked, snapping his tie.

"Positive."

He crawled across the bed and straddled my chest with his thighs, his warm ball sack resting in my cleavage.

"Pick up your head a bit. I don't want to get your hair," he said. He tied the tie across my eyes, shutting out the world from view. I already missed his amber eyes staring back at me.

"Can you see?" he asked quietly.

"No. This is a lovely tie by the way. It really brings out your eyes," I said, stroking the silky material across my face.

"Thank you." He paused before asking, "Is that hard for you?"

"Is what hard?" I was confused.

"Saying something nice to me." He stroked the back of his hand down my cheek.

"No. Why would you think that?" I tried to catch his hand, but he was gone.

"Gee, I have no idea, Skye."

He moved from on top of me, and I felt the bed dip and then level off again.

"Where are you going?" I asked.

"Nowhere. I'm right here." He touched my arm with his fingertips, letting me know he was near. With the tie across my eyes, though, I had no idea what he had planned. Silence filled the room, and I grew uneasy. I tried to focus on my breathing and staying calm. I knew rationally it was all part of the head game, but it was hard for a control freak like myself to stay in the right state of mind.

A few minutes passed, and I strained to hear what he was doing, but he moved like a panther. I heard nothing. I battled the urge to take the blindfold off and call the night a bust. My breathing accelerated, and I did my very best to calm my body.

Heat traveled to my face. I was getting more and more anxious the longer I lay there. It was utterly ridiculous, and I knew that. Nothing was even happening, and I was getting myself worked up. I tried to focus again on my breathing, counting the heartbeats I could hear thrumming in my ears, but it was no use. I couldn't concentrate.

"You need to settle down." His voice came from inches away. He'd probably been sitting next to me the entire time. But because he had been so quiet, I'd been convinced he had left me there, alone and naked on my bed, blindfolded and foolish, waiting for something that wasn't going to happen.

"I know you have a very strong mind," he said. "You need to put that beautiful brain to work *for* you, not against you." He was so close to my ear, I could feel his breath on my skin.

Of course, he was right, but I didn't want to hear it.

He pushed a few wayward strands of hair back behind my ear and let his fingers continue down my neck with a whisper-soft touch, over and over, in a hypnotic rhythm. Eventually he changed to a firmer stroke and then used his fingernails, scratching my scalp and skin lightly, making my skin come alive.

"Turn your back to me," he said, and I did as he asked, propping myself on my side. He must have been kneeling at the side of the bed, so I didn't have to go too far toward the center of the mattress.

Kyle touched my skin, just dancing lightly across the surface at first, building up to a firmer touch, and then transitioning into scratching. On my back he used something other than his fingernails, and I tried to figure out the object at first before giving in to the sensation. My entire body was a live wire by the time he was done.

When he slipped his hand between my thighs from behind and dipped into the wetness of my pussy, I heard his groan.

"Good girl. Such a good girl. I want to be inside you so badly, Skye."

"Then do it, Kyle. Fuck me."

"Are you ready now, Rocket? Or do you want me to pet you more?" he asked, his voice silky smooth.

"No, I need you now. Please. Please, Kyle. Fuck me now." I writhed on the mattress, arching my body so he could appreciate my feminine curves.

The bed gave way under his weight, and I felt the head of his cock nudging at my ass. He ran his fingers through my pussy again, slipping a finger into the opening and pressing deep inside.

"Oh, my God, yes. Feels so good." I moaned, fucking myself on his hand.

"Are you sore? Are you sure you want to?" He kissed my shoulder, biting and licking the same spot again and again.

"Yes. Please. Yes, I'm sore, but it will feel even better."

"Oh, my Rocket likes a little pain. I get it now. You are seriously a dream come true. Bend this knee forward." He tapped my top leg. Since I was still on my side, moving that way opened my sex to him completely.

The angle he entered me was perfection. I turned my face into the pillow and keened loudly. The muffled sound still filled the room.

"Jesus, Kyle." I panted. "Feels so good." I reached back and grabbed on to his thigh while he drove into me repeatedly. He was a different lover than the night before. This time he was more forceful and punishing, and I was on the verge of orgasm in short order.

I thrashed beneath him, needing something to anchor myself to. The position we were in left my entire torso twisting back and forth every time he smacked into me, and I needed leverage to absorb the impact.

"What is it? What do you need? Tell me," he issued more as a demand than a concern.

"I need to hang on to something. To push back. I can't fight back like this." I didn't know if what I was saying even made sense.

"All right." He swung my top leg high in front of his face and rested my calf on his shoulder. Now my back was flat on the mattress. Much more comfortable.

"Thank you." I sighed. "So much better."

"You good here?" He gripped the leg on his shoulder, checking that it wasn't too much for my lower back, and I nodded.

"Let me see you. Please." Suddenly I wanted the intimacy of looking into his eyes while he fucked me.

He pushed the tie off my eyes, and it took a few seconds for my sight to adjust to the dim light cast over my bedroom from the bathroom light.

"Are we good?" Sweat beads formed at his temple. He looked so sexy hovering above me.

"Yeah, we're good." I grinned up at him, pressing the side

of his face with my calf. He turned to the side and sank his teeth into my flesh, biting just to the point where I couldn't take it, then letting go.

When I swiveled my hips a bit, he took the hint and moved again, taking a slow pace at first, building up to a steady rhythm. He leaned forward to kiss me, and I met him halfway, blending demanding lips with passionate, wet tongues.

Having sex with Kyle Armstrong was quickly becoming one of the best things on the planet. So many sensations pummeled my brain that it was hard to focus on one singular thing. Drowning in the overall feeling was the better way to approach the experience. Just give in to the take-me-away sort of event. Later, when I lay in bed alone, I would overanalyze each singular detail.

Boy, would I ever.

"Are you close?" He panted between thrusts. "I can't wait much longer, I don't think. I'm trying, but your tight pussy is killing me."

"Yes! Yes. So close." I reached between my legs to rub my clit, a sure way to reach the finish line while he fucked me, and he batted my hand away. I glared up at him, but he was already shifting his weight to take the job on himself.

"Your pleasure is mine. Mine." He glared at me, daring me to argue back.

I closed my eyes and rode the wave. Something about the possessive talk ramped me up even higher.

"I'm coming, Kyle. I can't wait, can't...wait..."

"Right there with you. Do it. Let me feel you come on my cock, Skye."

My climax detonated through my body. An all-inclusive, limb-trembling, eye-rolling, mouth-drying orgasm to end all time.

Kyle jerked from my body and took his glistening cock in his fist and pumped several times before the milky semen spurted from the tip and splashed onto my belly and chest. He watched his marking, enraptured with his seed dripping down my skin, before releasing his cock to paint his fingers through it on my stomach.

I could not take my eyes off what he was doing, my pussy throbbing with arousal. I grabbed his hand and brought his fingers to my mouth, made eye contact with him, and sucked the sticky fluid off each one. He growled with a sound that was so animalistic, it made me want to offer myself to him again. There was something basic about him that spoke to something basic in me. And while it should've scared the shit out of me, it did the complete opposite.

At that moment, at least.

"You're so fucking perfect, Rocket," he said, watching me carefully. He probably already knew I'd freak out at any moment, put the full shield back up, and kick his ass out. Even though this was only our second time, the interactions in between should've been warning enough.

Before things got too heavy, he lay down beside me and pulled the covers up. I backed up into his side, and he turned to cradle me with his body. We lay quietly for a while before I finally broke the magic spell. "I don't care if you spend the night here, but you have to leave before the sun comes up, and that's pretty early," I said. "You may want to go now. There's no way either one of us can risk being seen like this."

"Skye, it's a city council seat, not vice president of the free world. Don't you think you're being overdramatic?" He drew lazy circles on my arm while he spoke.

I shrugged him off me. "No, I don't. I've watched good people get destroyed over less. You've been in the same world for the same amount of time. You know it's true." I sat up, clutching the covers to my chest, and twisted to glare at him.

"I don't know... It still seems silly."

"Silly?" I flipped on the light on the nightstand and gave him a dirty look. "Silly? Kyle, really? Silly?"

"Okay, settle down," he said. "Come on. Turn off the light and lie down. It's late. I didn't mean to get you all riled up." He spoke with a careful quietness like you would around a spooked horse.

Now I all but sprang out of bed and stormed into the bathroom for my robe. When I came back into the room, I was knotting the belt with such force I'd probably have to cut the thing off rather than be able to untie it.

"See? Here's the difference. Right here's the difference. You. And me."

He looked so confused I almost felt bad for him.

Almost.

"What the hell are you talking about?" He had his legs hanging off the side of the bed by that point, rubbing the back of his neck in frustration.

"I noticed it tonight for the first time. You're not really taking any of this seriously, are you? You didn't talk to any of the reporters at the dinner. Hell, outside of the woman from the teachers' union who kept following you around, you barely made the effort to talk to anyone. Why are you even running in this election?" My tone was nothing but accusatory, and I would probably regret it later, but my temper was flaring brighter than a flame being fed by an open fuel line.

"I've been asking myself the same thing."

"And then there's this!" I continued as I motioned frantically between us, likely looking as crazy as I was sounding. "This doesn't bother you for myriad reasons, least of which is the obvious."

"The obvious?" Kyle asked, raking his hands through his sex-mussed hair.

"Don't play dumb with me now, Counselor. To use your words, it really doesn't suit you. If you were to get caught sneaking out of here, the press would paint you as a sexy heartthrob getting his rocks off. Blowing off some good old red-blooded American steam, right? But If I get caught with you sneaking out of my place, what does the press do to me?"

He stared and didn't say a word. Probably because, like me today with Bailey, he knew the answer and knew it wasn't fair.

"What happens to me, Kyle?" I yelled, probably waking the neighbors who shared a wall with my condo.

"They'd paint you as a slut," he finally said, hanging his head with the admission.

"Bingo." I stared at him, waiting for him to say something. Anything.

But he didn't. Because there was nothing more to say.

"You need to leave. And we can't do this again." My voice

was filled with pain and resignation. The plain and simple truth was that I might be falling for this guy, and it just couldn't happen.

He stood. "I disagree—"

"Of course you do." I threw my hands up in frustration. Was none of what we were saying registering with him?

"What's that supposed to mean?"

"You have nothing to lose. I, on the other hand, stand to lose it *all*. I'm serious, Kyle. You need to get dressed and go. I don't want to spend the night with you." I couldn't be sure, but I thought there might have been actual tears forming in my eyes.

Real ones.

"You don't mean that. You're upset." He started toward me.

"No, I'm finally seeing things clearly. When I'm not under your magic golden-eyed sex spell and can think clearly. I need to keep my eye on the prize. My future. The future I've busted my ass for all these years. You, my sexy man, are not part of that. No man ever has been or probably ever will be."

"That sounds like a very lonely life, Skye. If that's what it means to be successful in this field, you can have it."

"Would you mind going on record with that concession speech, Counselor?" I said, trying my best to channel Bailey and slide that professional demeanor back into place like a mask.

He got up and put on his slacks and shirt. He draped the jacket over his arm and carried his shoes with him toward the door. "Aren't you even going to walk me out?"

"Nah. I'll lock up once you're gone. Good luck in the election, Kyle."

He looked at me and shook his head. Whether it was in disbelief or disgust, I wasn't sure. Either way, my chest felt like it was caving in on itself.

"You know, I really thought we could have had something."

"Timing's everything." I shrugged, clinging to my composure by my fingernails until he walked out the front door.

After the door closed quietly, I waited a minute or two to go and lock it. When I went back into my room, out of habit, I straightened the covers on my bed, and Kyle's gold-patterned tie tumbled to the ground. I picked it up and went into my closet and hung it neatly with my scarves and belts, running my hand over the pattern a few times before pushing the other clothing together around it so I wouldn't see it among my things. One day I would return it to him.

One day when I was ready to face all the feelings that went along with it.

With him.

One day...

CHAPTER EIGHT

From the moment the door closed behind Kyle, I launched into major self-analysis and self-improvement mode. On top of everything else that had happened, I was still beating myself up for lying to Bailey at lunch. Convinced she no longer trusted me, I composed a lengthy email regarding my character and cited several examples of why I could be counted on in the future. But in a huff, I deleted the entire thing before I could really embarrass myself by sending it.

Next, I hit the fridge for the emergency half gallon of salted caramel pretzel ice cream. I considered eating the entire thing, but I stopped about halfway through, knowing I'd be sick within an hour. Girls who were sensitive to dairy products regretted everything ice cream-related within an hour. Sure enough, I was soon moaning in pain, trying to distract myself from the misery by reading the latest post on one of my favorite fashion blogs, convinced none of my clothes would ever fit again by the looks of my bloated stomach.

"No pity for the self-induced body disfigurement," I preached to myself.

"It was worth it!" I yelled at my miserable reflection in the bathroom mirror. My reflection just stared back at me, looking, well...miserable.

Because I was alone.

Alone.

Eventually, exhaustion from all the extra emotions and the very long day won out, and I finally fell asleep. If I was very generous in my calculations, I logged almost three and a half hours of sleep. Browbeating was one of my superpowers, and I'd given myself a good whipping for most of the sleepless night. You name it, I'd covered it. From any potential missed opportunities at the dinner to what I'd said to Kyle.

When I stared in the mirror the next morning, the Zombie-Apocalypse survivor staring back at me had no right to complain. All self-induced. All well-deserved. To top it all off, I'd started my period. That explained a lot of the emotional roller coaster bullshit—and possibly the eating tantrum and stomachache—but the big golden-eyed elephant in the room would have to stay swept under the rug for now. I needed to leave for Bailey's, or I'd be explaining why I was both untrustworthy *and* unpunctual.

Awesome.

When I got to their house, Oliver answered the door, already dressed and on his phone. He motioned for me to come in, and I stood off to the side until he ended his call. From his side of the conversation, I gathered he was talking with Janine, his partner at Book Boyfriend Incorporated.

"Sorry about that," he said after ending the call. "Some mornings, Janine is on my case right out of the gate. I don't know what I'd do without her, but there are times I'd like her to bring it down a notch, you know?" He gave me a warm hug hello, and I really didn't want him to let go.

He leaned back while still holding me in his arms to give me a good once-over. "Hey, Skye Blue, you okay?"

"I'm okay." My voice was hoarse from being so dehydrated. "Long night."

"That fundraiser more fun than raiser?" He grinned, amused with his own joke.

"No, I wish that was it. I powered my way through a half gallon of ice cream and then paid for it in a bad, bad way." I clutched my stomach to illustrate the problem.

Oliver gave me a disapproving look. "You know better than that." He patted a stool at the end of their generous kitchen island. "What's his name?"

"Why do you go down that path first?" I climbed up on the stool and rested my head in my arms.

"Because you're my best friend and we lived together for a really long time. I've nursed you through a lot of douchebags, baby. Come on, I'll make you some coffee."

"Ugh." I groaned, holding my stomach while it did its own version of the sound.

"All right, how about some vitamin water? That usually helps."

I looked up to watch him mill around the kitchen. He looked perfectly in his element, and for the first time today, my heart felt something other than broken.

"Is Bailey here? She told me to be here first thing. Did I come too early?"

"Yeah, she's upstairs. She was on the phone when Janine called, so I came down here so we wouldn't be talking over one another." He set an orange-colored bottle in front of me.

"So how are things going? Between the two of you?" I asked, struggling with the lid.

"Things are great. I couldn't ask for more, really." He took the bottle from me and opened it easily. With a wink, he handed it back. "I'm crazy in love with her. We get along better than I've ever gotten along with anyone. I don't know what more I could want, you know?"

"Yeah, you're a lucky man. She's a lucky woman. I hope she's treating you well." I took a big gulp of the electrolyte drink and could feel it make its way down into my empty stomach.

"Of course I'm treating him well. Have you tasted his cooking?" Bailey walked into the kitchen, beaming at Oliver. They kissed when she got beside him, and I actually had to look away as my stomach clenched tight with jealousy.

"Right? I don't think I've had a decent meal since he moved out, other than when I get an invite to come over here. At least my waistline is grateful." Hopefully I'd recovered with a believable smile. It wasn't that I wasn't truly happy for them, because I was. It was just a harsh punctuation on what was missing from my life. What I kept trying to convince myself I didn't want.

"You look green. Are you sure you aren't coming down with something?" Oliver asked again, reaching over to feel my forehead with the back of his hand.

"No, I'm fine. It's Aunt Flo. She's a serious nuisance this month." That would end the conversation quickly. Oliver hated talking about female stuff more than anything.

"And there's my cue to leave." He turned back to Bailey. "I have to run a few errands this morning anyway. We have some costume props to pick up, so I need to run across town. Shouldn't be too long. Text me if you need anything. Okay?"

He kissed her on the forehead, and she closed her eyes and smiled while he did so. They were so sweet to watch I wanted to curl up in the fetal position on the floor and rock myself. I watched him walk out the back door of the kitchen and down the path to the detached garage behind the house.

"This really is a beautiful home, Bailey." The last time I had been over, it was dark, so I didn't get to appreciate the backyard. They had much more space than most homes in the neighborhood. "You scored on this lot size," I commented, peering out the windows along the back of the kitchen.

"Thank you. I wasn't sure I'd want to stay here after William died, but Oliver has made it so much more of a home than William and I ever did. I don't know"—she shrugged— "it just feels right." She looked at me. "Does that seem odd? I mean, sometimes I wonder what people think. Like I just moved one man out and another in. It all happened so fast. But we don't really get to pick how love happens in our hearts, do we?"

"No"—I sighed deeply—"I guess we don't." Boy, she couldn't have said truer words.

Not that I was in love with Kyle. Because I definitely was not. In love with him, I mean.

Not at all. Even a little.

Why was I arguing with myself so intensely?

"The lady doth protest too much, methinks."

I never did like Shakespeare.

I gave my head a slight shake when I realized Bailey was

staring at me. Maybe I'd trailed off midsentence again.

"I guess if I'm ever in that boat—in love, I mean—I'll let you know. I can tell you one thing, though. I've never seen him look so content or so at peace with himself than I did this morning when I walked through that front door." I pointed past her shoulder to the ebony door in their foyer.

"For some reason, that makes me very happy to hear," she said.

"Well, I'm guessing because his happiness is important to you? Not to mention no other woman has been able to accomplish what you have, so you definitely have something special."

"Tell me how the event went last night. Did you secure any more endorsements?" Social hour was over, and we switched gears to business without preamble. Typical Bailey style.

"It went really well, I think. I met a lot of voters, so that was great to get out and be among the people, so to speak. I sat with Jennifer Collette from the school board and Doug—oh shit, totally drawing a blank on his last name. I got his card. I have it in my purse. The guy from the water district. They were both very chatty and seemed to like what I had to say."

"But neither said you could count on their support? That's what you need to walk away with, Skye. Not just business cards. I can circle back with them via email, but it's so much harder for them to say no right to your face than it is for them to give me the brush off in an email. Make sense?" She leveled her stare at mine.

"Yes. Absolutely." I nodded in assurance. "I'll keep that in mind for the next one. When is the next event?" God, how I hoped she'd say tomorrow. I really wanted to go home and get back in bed.

"You have a ribbon cutting at a new strip mall at Third and Simpson at noon and a school board meeting tonight at six and then a dinner with the other candidates and the mayoral candidates at eight thirty." She scrolled through her calendar app confirming the events as she spoke.

"Jesus Christ, I'm exhausted just hearing about all that." I laughed, but Bailey was stone-faced.

"You know this is going to be the pace for the next month, right? Are you sure you're up for it?" Again, she laser-focused her stare at me. She'd make a scary mom someday.

"Yes. Of course! I was just joking. I can't be so serious all the time, Bailey. At least not around you and Oliver. It's not healthy for my brain. I need to let off steam somehow. And if I'm not going to be doing it any other way..." I trailed off, not wanting to open that can of worms with her again.

"Do I want to know what that last part means?" she asked, hiking her eyebrows up into her hairline.

"Nope." I put my drink to my lips to avoid saying anything more.

"You were with him again last night, weren't you?" she asked pointedly.

"You just said you didn't want to know. Why go digging for more?" I said after gulping down my drink.

"No, *you* said I didn't want to know," she clarified. "Now I definitely want to know, especially by that grin spreading across your entire face. This guy must be one hot number."

I folded my arms and buried my face in them. I was so

turned around where Kyle Armstrong was concerned, and I didn't feel enough of a warm, fuzzy connection with Bailey to really get into the details of it.

"Okay. Okay." She put her hands up in a gesture of surrender. "I get the hint. I said my piece on the subject yesterday. But I can tell the man has your knickers in a knot. If you need someone to talk to, I'm a pretty good listener. Of course, you always have Oliver. Don't feel like just because he's living here now, you can't come over and talk with him."

"I appreciate that, Bailey. I really do. I told Kyle last night we aren't going to be seeing each other again. Not that we're seeing each other." I made air quotes around *seeing each other.* "I mean, let's be honest. We're fucking. Hooking up. Booty-calling."

Again, she put her hand up to stop me. "I get it, Skye."

"But it's over. No more. *Nunca más,*" I said with conviction. Or what I hoped sounded like conviction.

"Are you trying to convince me or yourself?" she asked, finally sitting down on one of the stools at the island.

"Yes!" I smiled. "Back to business, though. Can you print out the calendar as it stands right now? Or share it with me on the cloud so it updates my calendar? I live by my phone. I mean, we all do, right? So, it would be really helpful to have these events at a glance, especially more than a day ahead of time."

"Absolutely." She made a quick note on her pad, which I had quickly come to learn meant it was as good as done. The woman was the most organized, methodical creature I'd ever met. I thought I had my shit together until I met Bailey Hardin.

Now I felt like a lovesick schlub.

No!

Rewind.

I was one hundred percent not in love with Kyle Armstrong.

Definitely not in love.

Lust. Yes.

Really, how could I not be? That bastard had moves I'd never felt before. He had ways of making the stars crash to earth and dance in my bedroom to his wicked pelvic drumbeat.

But definitely not love.

"You okay?" Bailey interrupted my inner argument.

"Hmm? Oh, yeah, sorry. Too little sleep last night. Seriously, my period came on like gangbusters, and I was up half the night with cramps and the whole nine yards. Of course, the half gallon of ice cream I powered through didn't help the stomach *sitch*."

She held her hand up again, like before, to stop me. "TMI, hon. Honestly."

"Do you ever just have a raw moment? Like ever?" This time, I was the one throwing down the stare.

"What is that supposed to mean?" She sounded offended.

"I don't know. You're always so carefully planned. So measured. Do you ever just blurt out exactly what you're feeling? With anyone? Don't you have a person you can do that with?" I asked, my tone easing up by the end of the question.

She thought for a few seconds, and it felt like a few seconds too long. For me, I would say instantly, of course, Oliver. Laura. Easy. But Bailey was really, really thinking about it.

"Well, I guess, Oliver? But it's just not my personality. I was raised this way, Skye. In a very uptight household. We didn't talk about *feelings*"—her face scrunched up when she said the word—"and share details of our feminine hygiene problems or bathroom mishaps. It just didn't happen."

"That's too bad, you know? It lets the steam out now and then. Plus, it lets the people around you know you're human. Not a robot. Makes you more approachable."

She still stared at me like the idea was foreign, so I continued. "Haven't you ever wondered why people sort of steer clear of you?" There. I said it.

"People don't steer clear of me." Bailey sounded defensive.

I tilted my head to the side a bit. "Okay."

"They don't. I mean, not really. People are just intimidated by me."

"Right. You're probably right. Well, I better shove off, I have a long day ahead of me, and I need to look better than this." I looked down at the jeans and T-shirt I'd thrown on carelessly. "Plus, I'll need to figure out how to do a wardrobe change somewhere on the road before the dinner later tonight."

"I can always meet you somewhere with clothing if you need me to," she said. "William used to change at some of the nicer hotels around town. The lobbies have clean and spacious restrooms, and if you get to know the front desk clerks, they're usually more than accommodating. If you want me to make some calls, just let me know," Bailey offered as we walked to the front door.

"I'll check in with you throughout the day and see how things are going. Make sure plans haven't changed," I said, stuffing my phone into my purse.

"Sounds good. Remember, you want commitments," she called as I went down the front walk.

"Right. Thanks, Bailey," I called over my shoulder.

"My pleasure. Bye." She gave a little wave before disappearing behind the closed door.

While I waited for my car to cool down a bit, I ran through my day's schedule again on my phone. The calendar I asked Bailey to sync up with mine had already come through, and I stared blankly at the last event. Why hadn't her words sunk in before? I had to see Kyle tonight at dinner? How was I going to keep playing this off?

Because I was professional and had worked too damn hard to get to this point. That was how. If I needed to write affirmations for myself and post them all over my belongings, I would do it. There was no way I would fuck this up because of a man. No. Way.

I rested my head on the steering wheel and fought back tears. Even this was ridiculous. I never cried. Ever. Why was Mother Nature screwing with me at the most inopportune time with an emotional monsoon menstrual cycle this month?

I selected Oliver on my *recently called* list and hit Call.

"Hey, you, what's up?" His upbeat voice made me smile.

"Can you talk? Are you busy?" I pulled out of their neighborhood and headed home.

"No, just stuck in fucking traffic. Don't get on the 101, whatever you do," he groaned.

"Ollie, no one with a brain gets on the 101. What were you thinking?" I teased. Seriously, everyone who lived in

Los Angeles knew to avoid that freeway at all costs. It was a nightmare twenty-four-seven. But at least I had a captive ear for a while.

"So what's up?" he asked.

"I need some advice. Or maybe just someone to talk some sense into me."

"It's funny you think I'm going to be the one to do that. Oh, how times have changed." He chuckled, and I didn't miss the irony of our relationship's role reversal. For as long as I could remember, I was the one who had dished out the advice, which Oliver had always duly ignored.

"I'm just going to get right down to it." When he didn't object, I continued. "I met someone."

"That's great, Skye. I'm glad to hear it. But why did you start this with me talking some sense into you? Are you already thinking of ways to sabotage your own happiness?" Oliver asked, not mincing words with me.

"What is that supposed to mean?" I asked, already frustrated.

"What is that supposed to mean?" He imitated my voice.

If he were sitting beside me, I'd punch him. Hard. "I hate when you do that, Oliver."

"I know. That's why I do it. Because that's your modus operandi, my love. You see a chance at happiness, and for whatever reason, you start undermining it before it has a chance to gain wings."

"I do not."

"Totally do. Every single time," he battled back.

"No, I don't," I insisted.

"Did you call to argue with me? Because we can do this all day. But you know I'm right. Think about the last guy. And not that Lando dipshit. He doesn't count." He laughed, and I couldn't help but chuckle too.

"Landis," I corrected.

"Good Christ. Landis. What kind of name is that?" he asked, still snickering a bit.

"You sound like Laura right now," I mumbled.

"Well, she's a smart girl. We both knew he was a waste of your time. But the one before him, the banker, shit...Chris? He was a good guy. But you chewed him up and spit him out." Oliver had my dating history cataloged like a big brother would.

"Well, there were more problems there than either of you knew about, so don't think you always have the whole picture." I didn't really feel like going into the details of how passive Chris was in the bedroom, that I could never get off, and how there was no way I could spend the rest of my life with a man like that. Why bother investing more time dating when a relationship wasn't going to have potential in the long run?

"I can respect that. But tell me about this new guy. Who is he? Where did you meet him?"

"Well, I guess I met him at school. Had classes with him at UCLA. Never really cared for him, cocky son of a bitch..." I trailed off at the end, but he heard me.

"Sounds like your cuppa so far." He laughed again. He really did know me better than anyone.

"Laura and I were at Itza's one day after work, and this guy came up to our table and just started talking to me, to us.

Then I couldn't get rid of him. Laura's pregnant, by the way." I knew that would throw him off the trail. Admittedly, it was a dirty tactic.

"Jesus Christ. Are you trying to make me have an accident? You don't just throw shit like that into a conversation like, 'oh, I hear it's supposed to rain later,'" Oliver shouted over my car's speaker system.

"Sorry. Sorry. There's no way to ease into that factoid, is there?" I asked, feeling guilty for freaking him out.

"Yeah, but what the hell? Pregnant, like with a baby? Shit. Who's the father? I take it this was an accidental thing?" His voice was still louder than necessary.

"Of course a baby. And you better not say a word to her about it when you see her. I don't know if she wanted the news out on the street just yet. She's actually carrying the baby for her sister and brother-in-law. You know, a surrogate?" I intentionally used a nice, calm voice, hoping he'd follow my example and settle down.

"Oh, well, that's better, I guess." He took an audible deep breath. "But shit...I can't imagine Laura as a mom. None of us are ready for that yet. Well, I might be, but not the two of you." His last comment caught me off guard.

"First off, she's not going to be the child's mother. She provides a healthy place for the baby to grow—when the baby comes out, she hands it over and walks away. The end. No motherhood for her." Now I sounded like Laura, giving the rehearsed speech.

"Damn, that's kind of harsh, no? How does a woman do that? Don't you all form a bond or whatever? Like, while the kid is in you?" he asked.

"Dude, like I know? But yeah, I don't know. I guess she had to have counseling and stuff before they would let her do it, to make sure she was stable enough to deal with it afterward. All I know, she's puking her guts out every morning, so she must really love her sister to be going through all that voluntarily." I honestly hated throwing up more than anything.

"What was the second thing?" he asked, seemingly at random.

"Huh?" I asked, ever so intelligently. Only with Oliver did I have the freedom to really be at ease.

"You said, 'first off,' as though you were going to list more than one thing," Oliver answered.

"Oh, right. Are you really ready to be a father? Don't you want to get married first?" The more we talked about other things, the less time I'd have to talk about Kyle. Now that I'd lifted the corner of the lid, I wasn't so sure I wanted to open the box in front of Oliver after all.

"Sure we do. I don't think we'll have an elaborate wedding or anything," he said. "I told her it was up to her. I'm not overly concerned about my family anymore, you know, about what they want. I've finally gotten off that nauseating merry-go-round."

"Good for you, Ollie. I'm so happy to see you so happy. It makes my heart feel full when I see you now."

"I want that for you too, Skye. I really do. Can this new guy be the one?" he asked, circling back to Kyle.

"Oh shit. I can't even see him in public. So that's totally putting the cart before the horse," I blurted out.

"Wait. I don't follow, at all. Why can't you see him in public?"

"He's running in the same damn race I am. I had no idea the first night we hooked up—neither of us did," I explained. "It's been booty call after booty call, basically. I haven't had a physical connection with someone like this, well, ever. For me, that's something. It's really important. But we can't explore it because it will destroy me professionally." I heaved out a sigh, really feeling the weight of the situation.

"Shit. That sucks."

"Yeah. That about sums it up."

"So now what?"

"I told him I don't want to see him anymore." I shrugged, even though Oliver couldn't see me.

"Of course you did."

"Again, what is that supposed to mean?" I felt like I was asking that a lot lately.

"Do you really not see it?" Oliver asked patronizingly.

"No, I guess I don't." I could feel my pulse starting to climb again.

"Every time you have even the smallest bump in the road, you kick the guy's ass out of the car. *Boom.* 'Get the fuck out.' You're such an all-or-nothing kind of girl. Life doesn't work like that. Ever. Relationships have bumps, Skye. A lot of them. You can't expect all newly paved roads all the time. You're going to be driving solo forever." His voice was sincere, and he wasn't trying to hurt me with what he said.

I was silent for a bit. I didn't have much to say in response because he wasn't wrong. But what did that say about me? Was

I afraid of commitment like he always accused me of? Most of the time he was playing around when he said it, but maybe there was truth to the jabs.

"Are you still there?" he asked, likely worried I might have hung up. Wouldn't have been the first time.

"Yeah, I'm here, just thinking," I said. "I do have to hang up, though. Just got home, and I need to make myself presentable for this ribbon cutting. But seriously, Oliver, it's like I said, even if we both wanted to see where things could go between us, we can't do it right now with this election going on. I'll be hung out to dry." It seemed like an impossible situation, no matter how I looked at it.

"Well, if you think it might be worth it, maybe you should have a talk with him," he offered. "Tell him where you're coming from and see if you can regroup after the election."

"That's pretty good advice, Oliver. You're turning into a real Dr. Laura." Now I was teasing him, but I also meant it.

"Don't ever say that again," he said, his voice full of mock warning.

"I love you. I'll talk to you later." I paused before saying, "Thank you."

"I love you too, Skye Blue. Bye."

The rest of the day flew by. Hauling my butt from one side of my district to the other and then back again hadn't seemed like it would be a big deal before I left work for the ribbon cutting midmorning. But adding the after-work rush hour on the way to the school board meeting and then the tail end of it again on the way to the dinner was a double punishment. No one in their right mind would sign up for doing this on a regular basis.

It was becoming obvious why so many city officials had drivers—so they could work in the back seat while stuck in traffic. I could make phone calls, but that was the extent of my productivity. I couldn't write anything down, so whatever call I did make couldn't be too heavy with detail or I would forget everything by the time I got to a light or a full stop to jot down notes. It was a monumental waste of time. I'd have to pick Bailey's brain on a better way to utilize the time behind the wheel, because if there was one, I was sure she knew of it.

Lloyd Jessup was present for the school board meeting, but Kyle was a no-show for both that and the ribbon cutting. So far, I was winning the attendance contest, at least. My nerves were a jangled mess, driving to the restaurant where we were meeting for the scheduled dinner. It was supposed to be a friendly, get-to-know-one-another type of thing in a private room at one of the nicer restaurants in our neighborhood, but Bailey said she wouldn't be surprised if the restaurant owner tipped off the press, so to expect a photo op.

Checking my hair and makeup one last time in my rearview mirror, I saw Kyle pull in right behind me and froze. We made eye contact in the mirror, so there was no way to dodge him. I sucked in a deep breath and said out loud, "You are strong. You are brave. You got this." A habit I got into doing sometimes in college when I needed a pep talk and no one was around. Sometimes a girl had to count on herself when the going got tough.

He opened my car door for me, and I swung my legs out first, knowing they looked damn good in the dress I'd chosen. A black sheath, flattering but not flashy, with a three- or four-inch keyhole opening at the décolletage, which added visual interest. Other than that, it was just black. I'd worn nude hose and a pair of black pumps. Classic, classy, and understated.

Kyle looked amazing as usual. The man had a great sense of style, and I met his gaze when he offered his hand to help me out of the driver's seat. I smoothed down my dress and sneaked a quick peek at his ass in his slacks as he closed the door.

"You look stunning," he said when he turned to find me gawking at his bum, his golden eyes nearly glowing in the light of the parking lot.

"Thank you. So do you. You dress very well—for a man."

"Three sisters. They rubbed off, I guess. You ready?" He motioned toward the restaurant.

"I just need to grab my bag off the back seat." I opened the back door and grabbed the clutch, which I had haphazardly tossed things into while stuck in traffic. Hopefully I hadn't forgotten anything important.

"That should do it. Thank you for waiting for me. You didn't have to do that." I smiled politely, locking the car and dropping the keys into my bag.

"I wouldn't leave you in a dark parking lot by yourself, Skye," he said. "I care about you, if you haven't figured that out." He stopped walking and stared at me.

I quickly looked around. The last thing we needed was some reporter lurking around, hoping to pick up a scoop.

"We need to be discreet here," I said in a hushed voice. "My CM said she thinks the press will probably be here."

He threw his hands up, clearly frustrated I didn't take the bait on the tender moment. "Right, right. All about appearances with you. How could I forget?"

"Don't be like that." My shoulders slumped, and I wanted to rewind the moment. I hadn't meant to hurt him.

"Like what? It's the truth, isn't it?" His voice was gaining volume.

"You don't have to make it sound like I'm an ice queen, do you?"

He shrugged, and it jabbed my heart.

"We need to have a talk when we're in private," I said quietly as we walked toward the front entrance.

"Do we? I think you said all there was to say already. I mean, how many more ways do you want to gut me?" he said, his voice serious. "I was being a gentleman by walking in from the parking lot with you. I don't expect it to mean anything more." He reached for the front door, and I stopped him, putting my hand on his arm.

"You're really being a jerk right now," I whispered.

"That's funny, coming from you. Well, here we are. Smiles on." He plastered on a fake smile and pulled the door open. The rest of the guests were standing just inside the entry, waiting for us to arrive. I felt like dashing to the bathroom and crying.

But I didn't. Of course I didn't. I plastered on my practiced smile too and did my best to knock them all dead. All night long, I amped up the charm and made sure I was the best version of me I could be.

But it was definitely a challenge with Kyle sitting directly across the table from me for the entire night. Staying focused on the conversation going on around me rather than being transfixed by the way he handled his silverware with those skillful fingers that had been inside my body. Or responding to the same set of questions I'd been asked multiple times today when I could drift off listening to the baritone melody of his voice telling the man beside him a story from his childhood. By the time dessert menus were being offered by the waiters, I had to excuse myself to use the ladies' room just to splash cold water on my face and put some physical distance between me and the man I swore I wouldn't tumble into bed with again. At the moment, I couldn't think of a single thing I'd rather be doing.

CHAPTER NINE

The dinner was done by eleven, and we left in random groupings. I broke off to use the ladies' room one last time before getting on the road. The waiter had refilled my iced tea plenty, and I'd never make it home without having to stop otherwise.

The parking lot was almost empty, other than my car and Kyle's. A few other cars were on the apron of the lot, where I assumed the employees were instructed to park to leave the premium spots for patrons. Kyle emerged from the shadows when I stepped a few feet from the exit, nearly scaring me out of my skin.

"Jesus Christ!" My voice went up two octaves. "If I had pepper spray, you would be blind right now! Idiot!"

"Pepper spray wouldn't be necessary," he said. "You could screech someone to death like that." He wiggled his fingers in his ears.

I came to a grinding halt, planted my hands on my hips, and stared at him. "Did you need something? Come up with another clever insult you just couldn't let simmer until morning? Go ahead." I gestured wildly in the air. "Let's hear it. Get it off your chest, big boy, because I'm really tired."

"Don't be like that." He extended his arm toward me, but

I yanked out of reach.

"Don't be like that? Don't be like that?" I repeated, my voice so loud it bounced off the old buildings. "I'm getting whiplash over here, Armstrong."

He stuck his fingers in his ears again, like he was clearing them of something, shaking his head slightly. "*You are?*" His eyebrows climbed toward his hairline. "Such a hypocrite, Skye." He lewdly looked me from head to toe then. "Sexy as hell, but a hypocrite all the same."

"Hypocrite? Me?" I was nearly shouting in frustration.

"You need to keep your voice down," he warned, taking a step or two closer to me.

"You think I'm sexy?" I made a slash in the loose gravel with the toe of my pump, not wanting to look him in the eye when I asked.

"You know I do. And I would say by the way you were eye fucking me all night, the feeling is mutual." His answering voice was rough with arousal, and he took another step in my direction. "This dress. I just—yeah. This dress." He stalked closer, and I put my hand up to stop him.

"Kyle. We can't do this anymore."

"You keep saying that." His body was almost against mine by then.

"Then why aren't you listening?" I tilted my head back to look up at his scruffy jaw.

"Neither of us wants that." He circled his arms around my waist and pressed his forehead to mine. "Follow me." The first time he said the words, they were quiet, but as the plan seemed to firm, along with his cock I could feel pressing against me, he said more confidently, "Follow me in your car." Then he backed away a few steps.

"Where to?" I sounded like a love-struck teenager.

He had turned away completely and walked toward his car. He said without looking back, "To my house."

"No! I said no more." I stammered for just one second, trying to think of a more convincing reason. "Plus, I started my period." Yes, ladies and gentlemen, I just shouted that across a deserted parking lot. Excellent.

"So?" He opened his door, finally looking at me.

"So?" I asked in disbelief. Wasn't that the universal deal killer?

"That's what I said. So?" He flashed that irresistible sex-soaked grin. Then, just before ducking into the driver's seat, he said, "You have a mouth, don't you?"

As if proving his point, I dropped said mouth open in shock. Nothing came out at first. Then, "I hate you so much."

"No, you don't. Follow me." And he started his engine.

I got in my car, still processing what I'd just heard and arguing with myself about what I should do. I could pull out of the lot and look like I was following him but turn toward my house instead.

But he and I needed to have a serious conversation if there was a chance in hell we could make things work between us. If, and that was a big *if*, that was what he still wanted. After the way I had spoken to him over the past twenty-four hours, there were definitely hurt feelings, bruised egos and, possibly, matters of the heart to be atoned for.

The streets were free of traffic due to the late hour, and

my mind darted back and forth between possibilities. Before I could decide on a different plan, Kyle turned into the driveway of a modest one-story home. I looked for nearby parking on the street and was lucky to find something a few houses away. I parked and rested my head back on the seat.

Was this really the best idea? Moreover, why did I have so little willpower where this man was concerned? I continually said one thing and then did another. Lately, my resolve was taking one hit after another.

Kyle opened my door, scaring the shit out of me for the second time tonight.

"Christ, you need to stop doing that." I put my hand over my thumping heart and looked up at him.

"Being a gentleman? I think you've been hanging out with the wrong guys." He smirked, knowing damn well that wasn't what I meant.

"No, scaring me half to death." I released the safety belt and got out but then bent back into the car to unlatch the trunk to retrieve my duffel bag with the change of clothes from earlier. They would come in handy if I decided to spend the night. While I was bent over, Kyle grabbed on to my hips and ground himself into my ass. My eyes fell closed, and I absorbed the pleasure of his erection rubbing against my sex through my dress.

"My new addiction," he said coarsely, replacing his groin with his hand, pressing his middle finger in deeper than the others, zeroing in on the crack of my pussy lips.

Standing abruptly when I realized someone could be watching, I smacked the back of my head on the doorframe of my car.

"Fuck! Goddammit!" I yelped, rubbing my skull. "Shit!" I looked at my hand to make sure I wasn't bleeding. "Fuck, that hurt." My eyes filled with tears from the pain.

"Let me see," he said, trying to help with my self-induced injury. "Let me see. Move your hand." He parted my hair away from the area. "It doesn't look like you broke the skin. You'll probably have a good bump, though. Let's go inside. I'll get you some ice."

He stroked my hair away from my face, trying to right the mess he'd created. "I'm so sorry." He looked directly into my tear-filled eyes and placed his palm tenderly against my cheek. "I didn't mean for that to happen. Obviously. What do you need from the trunk? I'll grab it."

Thankful to break the moment and not have Kyle watch actual tears track down my cheeks, I reached back into the car to grab my purse off the driver's seat while answering, "I have a bag in there with some clothes. More comfortable than this," I said, not wanting him to assume I was spending the night.

He was already around the back of the car, looking through the trunk. Like the rest of my world, it was neat and organized, and the bag was right in plain view.

"This red-striped one?" he asked anyway.

"Yeah. Thank you for getting it. I can carry it, though. My head is fine." I stretched my hand out to take the bag from him, but he swatted it away.

"I got it. You concentrate on not hurting yourself on the way to the front door."

"Ha! Very funny," I said, following him up the driveway.

Kyle's home was very quaint. Built-in niches took the

place of bulky furniture, other than a sofa and coffee table in the living room. The absence of an enormous television as the centerpiece of the seating area scored him major points in my book too.

It was an older home but newly remodeled. The décor was very masculine and uncluttered, a style I appreciated. Most of all, it was clean—spotless, more like. A man after my own heart.

"Your home is lovely. Just you here?" I asked, turning in a full circle in the middle of the main room, getting a view of the living space.

"Yep. I kind of prefer it that way. As you said at your place, I like the quiet after a long day. The street is a little too busy for my preference, but other than that, I'm really happy here. Neighbors are great, construction is solid." He looked around the room, nodding his head. "Yeah, I like it here."

"Have you always lived in California?" I asked, setting my purse down on the sofa.

"No. I came to this crazy state for college. I grew up in New Jersey, if you can believe that. Can I get you something? Drink? Ice for the noggin?"

"No, it's fine, really." I touched the spot and winced but quickly suppressed my reaction. "And they gave me so many iced tea refills during dinner. I'm going to be wired all night," I added, quickly changing the subject.

He came into the living room where I was standing and motioned to the sofa and loveseat. "Let's have this talk you keep insisting we need to have. You look like you're going to crawl out of your skin if we don't, so let's get down to it." Kyle sat on the sofa, and I sat on the loveseat so we were facing one another.

I breathed in and out a few times, trying to calm my nerves. It was literally now or never. I could let this man slip through my fingers because I didn't have the courage to put my feelings out there and see if he returned them, or I could be brave and own it all and let fate take the reins from there.

"Skye?" He was grinning when I looked up from studying my tangled fingers in my lap.

"Sorry." I chuckled. "I'm not very good at this kind of thing." I blew out my breath through pursed lips.

He leaned forward and put his large hand over mine. "You said you have your period, so we're already off the hook from having the worst conversation we could possibly be having right now. We're not prematurely becoming parents. Say what you want to say, and we'll go from there."

"I like you," I blurted out.

All the rehearsed poetic ramblings I'd come up with about feelings growing like a seed blossoming into a beautiful flower when nourished by the good times and bad, the sun and the rain—yeah, gone. My words spewed out like verbal vomit.

"I like you too," he said, smiling broadly.

I stared at him, sitting there looking devastatingly handsome in his dress shirt and slacks. Just him, staring back at me—that fucking grin making my pulse quicken.

"Is there more?" he finally asked, golden eyes dancing with mischief.

"That's really a lot for me," I said, gulping down the lump that was quickly forming in my throat.

Again, he took my hands in his. "Okay. Breathe, beautiful. Thank you for telling me how you feel. I appreciate your courage. I hear you saying that didn't come easily." He cocked his head toward me. "Do you want to say something else? You still look like you have this whole drama playing out in your mind."

"How do you do that?" I exhaled sharply again, feeling a bit off-kilter.

"Do what?"

"Seem to read me so well?"

"I just pay attention," he offered easily. "I'm interested in you. I take notice of things. The way you move, the way you breathe...or don't breathe." He winked at me. And while winking annoyed me in general, in this case it was adorable.

"I've been watching the way your eyes dart around the room. The way you shift your weight in your seat. Cross and uncross your legs. You matter to me"—he shrugged, as if every other person did those things—"so I pay attention."

My forehead was creased with dismay.

I matter to him? He's interested in me?

I couldn't recall the last time a man said something like that to me. Oh, wait, I could recall it, actually.

Never.

"Yeah. I really like you," I said again, grinning while exhaling fully, feeling safer with the admission.

His smile took over his whole face then, and he lifted my fingers to his mouth, but I quickly pulled back.

"Oh no. You keep that mouth away from me," I warned with a sideways glare.

He twisted his face in confusion.

"Until we're done talking, because I can't think straight when your mouth gets too close to my body. Apparently, any part of my body."

He laughed then, and it was so sexy I literally whimpered. Where the hell had this man come from?

"We need to set some ground rules first." I sat up straighter, ready to outline the things I had come up with. While the poetry was easy to discard, rules were my specialty.

"Oh, here we go." He flopped back against the sofa cushions and rolled his eyes.

"I'm serious." I swatted his thigh. "Kyle, this election—"

"Fuck this election!" He bolted upright. "I'll withdraw if that's what it takes."

"Don't be ridiculous."

"I'm not joking. I'm done." He shook his head vehemently. "I'm not going to do the shit we did tonight. Treating each other like we're not even in the same room all night. That sucked. Having to watch those other men drool over you all night?" He looked like he had bad gas pains. "I wanted to kick that one guy's ass by the time we left."

"What guy? No one was drooling over me. You're being silly."

"I'm not. One of the waiters. Why do you think your bladder's about to burst?"

"God, speaking of that, can I use your bathroom please?" I grabbed my purse from the end of the sofa while he directed me.

"Sure, second on the left." He pointed to the hallway

off the entryway, and I went to freshen up, take care of lady business, and collect my thoughts in solitude. I took a few minutes to brush my hair, careful to go gently over the bruise. I was definitely going to have a bump for a day or two.

When I came back to the living room, Kyle was sitting right where I'd left him, flipping through screens on his phone.

"Everything good?" I asked conversationally, sitting back down on the loveseat.

"Yep, just clearing email. Work won't seem to give me a break right now. We have a couple of big cases coming up, so it's hitting me from every angle. Jury selection for two big cases I'm on should be tomorrow or the next day, so the DA's having puppies."

"I'm not really helping, am I?" I asked sheepishly.

"What do you mean?" He tossed his phone onto the end table.

"Oh, just being female. With *feelings* and whatnot." I waved my hand randomly through the air.

"Don't be ridiculous. Come sit with me here." He patted the cushion next to him.

I smiled shyly and went to sit beside him. He immediately slung his arm around my shoulder and pulled me up against him. "Much better. It was too hard to look at you all the way over there and not be touching you. I had to deal with that bullshit all night."

"What if we just tough it out through the rest of the election?" I drew zigzags on his leg with my finger while I spoke. "I mean, think about it. It's only a few more weeks, and then we'll be free to explore what we have going on here without having to worry how it might hurt us. Or me, rather."

"I can't stay away from you for twenty-four hours. Unless you haven't noticed." He buried his nose in my hair and rubbed from side to side.

"I've noticed. And it's not a one-way street unless *you* haven't noticed."

"How do you propose we make it through three weeks? And I have news for you, Rocket. People who are trained in kinesics will see right through what's going on between us. Politicians are hiring body and language experts as coaches and advisors—to help them bring down the competition," he said, sounding serious. "I don't think we can pull it off, personally. I don't know about you, but my poker face isn't that great."

"That's unfortunate, isn't it?" I laughed.

"What?" Kyle asked, perplexed.

"You study body language yet can't fool people with yours?"

"Trust me, the irony isn't lost on me. But I think part of being good at tricking people is being good at being deceitful. That is something I'm not. Never have been."

"I really appreciate that," I told him. "I can't handle being lied to. In all things, even the tough stuff, I need the truth. It's what you will get from me, and it's what I expect in return."

"This is turning out to be a really bad time, career-wise, for me to have launched a political campaign," he said. "In all seriousness, I may pull out of the race. It would take care of the problem between us and free up time I don't have to spare."

"I don't want to be the cause of you giving up something you've always dreamed of. I couldn't live with myself. You would always resent me." I thought for a second and then added, "That's no way to start a relationship. I mean, if that's what we're talking about doing here."

While I was talking, I noticed a little wooden stool across the room, nestled in the corner. There were hand-painted designs on the top and down the short little legs. It was so intriguing, I stood to go look at it. "What is this little stool? It's adorable. Do you have a niece or nephew?" I looked back over my shoulder to ask while picking it up.

Kyle sat forward on the sofa while I went across the room.

It was child-sized, and on the top, painted in block letters, it read Kyle Marcus.

"Awww, this was yours from when you were a boy?"

"My grandmother used to paint as a hobby. Little plaques and figures. Tole painting, I think she called it?" His smile changed in depth as he remembered his family. "She made that when I was born, and I've had it ever since. I keep it there to remind me of her. She was instrumental in helping shape the man I am now."

"November eleventh? That's your birthday?" I asked in disbelief.

"It is. Veteran's Day baby."

"Me too!" I looked at him, grinning. What were the odds? Two babies born on the exact same day, a country apart.

"Oh boy. Two Scorpios. This could be a real disaster," he said, his demeanor shifting again.

"Or real fireworks," I pointed out. Astrology was my guilty pleasure. "Well, this is a real treasure. What did you use it for when you were a boy?" I loved getting to know him better.

"It was the naughty corner stool," he said, eyeing me carefully.

"Oh no! Were you a naughty little boy?" I teased but noticed he wasn't smiling anymore.

He shrugged. "I had my moments." He stood while he was talking and prowled toward me. The look in his eyes had darkened, and my breath hitched when I noticed. I'd definitely seen that look before. A plan was unfolding in his mind, and I could feel the air shifting around him.

"Maybe you should sit on the naughty stool for the way you tortured me tonight at dinner?" He cocked his head to the side in a challenge.

"I didn't torture you," I said meekly. Jesus Christ, this guy played dirty. "Now you're just making stuff up so you can punish me."

"Are you complaining?" He raised one eyebrow while asking. When I shook my head, he continued carrying out his devious plan.

"Put the stool on the floor in front of you, Rocket." He strolled leisurely across the room and dimmed the lights slightly, expecting me to do what he said while his back was to me.

I was straightening to stand from setting the stool down when he turned to face me. "Thank you for not making me say it twice. How does that dress open?" The nature of his words was conversational but direct.

Now, I just stared blankly. Not that it was a trick question; my mind seized up somewhere between trying to figure out what he had in mind and the fact that he knew I had my period.

I really thought tonight we'd just talk, maybe I'd sleep over, maybe cuddle—

"Skye!"

"What!" I jumped. "What?"

"The dress."

"There's a zipper. In the back." I looked at him, confused.

"Take it off and sit on the naughty stool and wait for your punishment." He winked and folded his arms across his chest. I'd have to be blind to miss the erection straining at the fly of his slacks.

Well, two could play this game. Because what he didn't know—I had on a very sexy thong, bra, and garter belt set that he would wish he didn't have to stare at and not be able to relieve himself afterward. I reached under my hair and unzipped the dress as far as I could on my own, struggling but not wanting to ask for help.

My usual bit, in other words.

Kyle stepped behind me to finish the job. "Lift your hair."

I did as he told me, and he slid the zipper to the middle of my back, exposing the black lace bra.

"Nice," he said, running his finger under the lace while kissing my shoulder and moving up my neck. I let my eyes close to enjoy the punishment. It was hell getting in trouble, after all.

Too soon, he was gone, walking around to stand in front of me. He made a motion with his hand, signaling for me to undress, so I let the dress slide down my arms, exposing my bra fully. I made sure to lock eyes with him for the next half. I wanted to see his reaction to the garter belt in particular. The nude thigh-highs clipped to the black lace straps of the garter belt on the fronts and backs of my thighs, making sexy arrows that pointed the way to Nirvana.

The dress dropped to the ground, and Kyle's groan filled the room.

"Fucking hell, Skye. Really?"

Going for the innocent bit, I said, "You don't like?" I looked down at my body and then back up to his face.

He was staring so intently, he didn't even respond. He reached into his slacks at the waistline to adjust his cock, and I couldn't help but giggle. I quickly bit my cheek, though, as to not poke the beast.

"Are you trying to kill me? Stroke me out from lack of blood supply to my brain?" he grated.

"No." I shook my head slowly. "You were the one who wanted me to take the dress off." I twisted at the waist to see where he had set my bag. "I have other clothes—"

"Stop."

I mashed my lips together and turned back to face him.

"Sit down." He watched me lower carefully to the seat of the stool, offering his strong hand for assistance. "Jesus Christ. I'm never going to look at that stool the same way again." He shook his head while walking around to stand behind me.

I heard the jangling sound of his belt buckle being unfastened just behind my head. Then, in one continuous *swoosh*, he yanked the leather strap free from his slacks' belt loops and dropped down to one knee behind me.

"Give me your hands," he instructed.

"Wha—?"

"I'm not speaking a foreign language here, babe."

Slowly, I put my hands behind my back like a person being led away in handcuffs by a police officer. "Were you restrained in the naughty corner when you were a child?" I squeaked, afraid to hear the answer. I really didn't want to know that he was abused as a little boy.

"No, of course not. This is my kinky twist on the process." He looped the leather around my wrists and slid the tongue through the buckle and secured the belt in place. "Okay here?" he asked, kissing my shoulder.

I tugged on the belt with my wrists, definitely not going anywhere. "It's fine."

"Let me know if you get uncomfortable. I'll take it off." He continued to kiss my shoulder and neck, moving my hair to the side and traveling up to just below my ear. He had such a fabulous way with his mouth and tongue, I quickly forgot I was being punished again.

Kyle came to stand before me, though far enough away that I didn't have to crane my head back too far. He kept his cat eyes locked on mine while he pulled the tails of his dress shirt from his slacks and unbuttoned each button and then finally took it off.

"You're so beautiful," I said to him, looking at his fit body.

"Thank you. But pretty words won't make it better," he said gruffly, staying in the mood of the punishment.

"I was giving you a compliment. Not trying to get out of whatever punishment you think I deserve." I rolled my eyes at the idea of needing to be punished. The sexy game was great and all, but I hadn't actually done anything.

"Did you just roll your eyes at me?" His voice dropped lower.

"Uhhh, I guess? Is that also a punishable offense?" I challenged.

He opened his pants and pulled out his very hard cock. "What do you think, Rocket?"

"Yes, I did roll my eyes!" I said enthusiastically, staring at his dick eagerly.

He stepped up in front of me. The height of the little stool put my mouth at the perfect height to receive his cock. "Open."

I licked my lips, almost out of instinct, and then opened my mouth.

"Open more," he said, holding his cock just in front of my mouth, taunting me with the proximity.

After I opened my mouth wider, he took a step closer, put one foot between my spread legs, and rested the head of his dick just inside my lips.

"Don't close until I say," he issued, taking my chin between his thumb and forefinger.

I raised my stare up at him, desperate to plead with him in some way. The urge to wrap my mouth around his shaft was so strong it was hard to hold back.

"I know, Rocket. I know. It goes against everything your body wants to do. You're doing an amazing job, though. Look at you. So sexy. God damn, so sexy."

He fed his cock in deeper, still holding my lower jaw open with the other hand. His tip was touching the middle of my tongue, and I began to salivate. I could barely taste him up to that point, but his scent was starting to fill my nose from inside, and I wanted to be completely surrounded by it. I closed my eyes and concentrated on what I could enjoy.

"Good girl." He moved his cock back and forth over my tongue, side to side in my mouth but not in deeper, which was what I wanted more than anything. I still had my eyes closed and focused on breathing through my nose. The whole experience was becoming overwhelming, and my breathing accelerated. The loss of control was one of the hardest things for me to deal with.

"Skye. Look at me again." Kyle read my body immediately. I looked up to him as he let go of my chin. I didn't close my mouth around him, and he beamed. "Very nice, baby. Very nice. Do you want to suck it?"

I nodded marginally, and his eyes drooped closed. "Do it, girl. Suck me."

I closed my lips around his shaft and wet the entire girth with my tongue. So much saliva had pooled in my mouth, he was coated instantly. I bobbed back and forth on him several times with my eyes closed, savoring the feel, the taste, and smell. I clamped my thighs together, wishing so desperately there was a way to get some sort of relief for myself as well.

Kyle groaned from low in his throat while his hips picked up the rhythm of my movement. After a minute, he said, "Be still for a second, Rocket." He put a hand on either side of my face, stopping my movement. I sucked a deep breath in through my nose, and he withdrew from my mouth completely.

"What's wrong?" I looked up at him. "Tell me. I'll do it differently." I wanted to please him, and the only way I would know how was if he told me.

"Nothing's wrong at all. That's the problem. I don't want to come yet. Just need to settle for a second." He bent over at the waist and kissed me roughly, yanking my head back by a fistful of my hair.

My moan filled our mouths while we kissed. He thrust his tongue into my mouth, tongue-fucking me deeply so I stopped trying to duel back with my own and just let him spear me repeatedly. When he pulled away, I looked up to him with dazed wonder.

How did I happen upon this incredible creature? How did I manage not to scare him off? Despite my normal tricks and usual self-sabotaging tactics—as Oliver so keenly pointed out—he was still as interested in me as I was in him.

Now, all I could think was, how did I get him to stay?

This was the point—or really close to the point—I normally cut bait and ran. I never saw a relationship past a month or two. I guess I'd had a few that went on for several months, but usually because the guy was out of town on a two-week assignment or something like that. I never managed to make it last that long on my own.

Kyle stood tall in front of me again and then took two steps back. "Spread your legs. Put your feet flat on the floor and swing your knees out, nice and wide."

I complied without hesitation and was rewarded with his groans.

"Mmmm. Yeah. Perfect. God, Rocket. So fucking sexy."

Since I still wore my heels, my knees were up higher than my ass on the low stool. The position gave my dirty coach a bird's eye view of all my goodies, for sure. I kept my eyes on his feet, suddenly feeling self-conscious.

"Look at me."

Lifting my gaze, I met his ocher stare and held it for a few seconds before he spoke.

"Do you wear lingerie like this every day under your work clothes? When I've seen you at city hall, you've had something like this right beneath your clothes?"

I watched his throat work as he swallowed the thought. The masculine bob of his Adam's apple beckoned me as surely as the erection straining from his hips.

"No. Not every time," I said. "Depends on my mood."

He rose to his full height before answering. "Interesting." He stepped out of his dress shoes and kicked them off to the side and then dropped his slacks as unceremoniously. They joined the shoes in a pile near the end of the sofa. His boxer briefs followed shortly behind.

I couldn't take my eyes off him, now naked other than the argyle dress socks bunched down at his ankles. A grin spread across my lips because he somehow still managed to look ridiculously sexy in just a pair of socks.

"Something amusing, Ms. Delaney?" he asked, dropping down to his haunches in front of me.

"I like your socks. They suit you," I said with a smirk.

He looked down as if he had forgotten which pair he put on that morning and then back up to my waiting smile. "Thanks. My mom gave them to me for my birthday last year. Along with the belt." He motioned with his chin past my shoulder to where I was still restrained.

"Excellent. A family affair, then. The stool, the belt. This isn't creepy. Honest." I raised my brow but quickly lost the joking spirit when I saw where his hand was headed. "Hey, captain. You don't want to poke around in there too much." I had a tampon in, but I wanted to remind him in the event he had forgotten.

"You let me worry about that. 'Kay?" He slid his finger along the side of the crotch of my thong. "Jesus Christ. Do you have any idea what this does to me? Feeling how wet you are?" His finger grazed my clit, only enough to tease me, but I was so amped up, it was electrifying.

I let my head fall back on my shoulder blades, which were pulled together tightly from the position of my hands at the base of my back.

"God, that feels so good," I offered to the ceiling.

He rubbed my clit more firmly from the outside of my panties and groaned. "I'll be right back." He stood and left the room.

I wanted to protest, but really, what was I going to say?

He was back within a minute with what looked like a blanket under his arm. He unfolded it and laid it on the floor in front of me, and then he got behind me and worked on unbuckling the belt.

"Try to not let your arms fling forward when this comes off, okay? I'll do my best back here, but I know how stubborn you are. With everything."

"Okay. I appreciate the heads-up." The belt gave way, and his hands were immediately around my wrists to control the pace at which my arms came forward. My shoulders protested slightly, but it wasn't too bad. I didn't exercise like Oliver, but I wasn't terribly out of shape either.

Kyle rubbed up along my arms and paid particular

attention to my shoulders. "How's that? You okay? How's the head, by the way?"

"I'm good. Really. I'm good." I was still perched on the little stool when he came back around to my front.

"As sexy as these are, let's give your feet a break, too." One by one, he slid my shoes off and carefully set them on the pile by his clothing. "The rest of this, however"—he motioned up and down my body, referring to the black lace lingerie—"stays."

He put his hand out to help me stand. "Your time on the naughty stool is up for tonight. Come lie by me." And then he escorted me to the center of the blanket he'd laid out. I didn't ask why we weren't going to his bedroom, because the whole setup was pretty cute the way he was working it.

He eased me down onto the soft blanket and followed with his own body immediately. Finding my mouth with his, he went to work with the drugging kisses I was beginning to need like air. I threaded my fingers through his hair and held his mouth to mine. I didn't want the night to end.

He moved down my neck to my breast, pulling my bra to the side so he could lick and suck my nipple into his mouth. When that wasn't enough, he nipped and fully bit me until I cried out in pleasure or pain or some combination of both. I chanted his name and made up new ones for him too.

Kyle traveled farther down my body to the sensitive flesh of my stomach, bringing me pleasure in ways I never knew possible. He made a trail from one side of my body to the other, worshiping and marking me in any way he saw fit, and I was happy to let him. He neared the juncture of my thighs, and warning bells signaled in my brain, but my libido shut them down.

He knew the situation. He was a grown man, and it wasn't my duty to teach him about Mother Nature. Then there was the fact that overshadowed all of the above—Mr. Armstrong was a kinky motherfucker. If he wanted to put his face in my pussy, knowing I was on my period, that was on him. I knew I was fresh. I made sure of it when I was in the bathroom before we started these reindeer games. Outside of the wetness from being aroused, he shouldn't encounter anything he didn't usually encounter in that zone.

Sure enough, he moved into position between my legs. He looked up my body to see me watching him and hovered just above my pussy. "Are you kidding? You're not going to freak out?" he asked in a deep voice layered with a challenge.

"That's all on you, big boy. You know what you're doing. Just make it happen already." I lifted my hips, pushing my crotch right into his mouth.

Big mistake.

He bit into my pussy with his entire mouth—all teeth— everywhere.

"Okay! Okay! I'm sorry. Sorry! Let go, Kyle!" I tried to push at his head, but that was a dumb idea because teeth dragging across your pussy parts was way worse than teeth clamping into your pussy parts.

The pain ramped up the pleasure exponentially, bringing me to the edge of climax quickly. Sucking him off plus all the kissing and touching had me so hot that by the time he put his mouth on me, I was halfway there already. Even without the added sensation of penetration, I was teetering on the verge of a fantastic orgasm. My panting and desperate grasping at his hair and shoulders should have clued him in that I wasn't going to be able to hold back much longer, but he wouldn't ease up. Finally, I threw my head back and wailed his name, my release crushing my composure completely.

At least I knew he didn't share walls with any of his neighbors.

"I need to fuck you. So badly, Skye. I need to be inside you." He stroked his cock while I watched, my head spinning from the endorphins surging through my system from the orgasm he just gave me.

"It's your call," I said, barely able to tear my eyes from his groin.

"Go." He motioned over his shoulder to the bathroom. "Hurry back."

I scampered to my feet and fought the headiest dizzy spell when I stood up. Still, I rushed to the bathroom to discard the literal cock-blocking tampon. I did a quick cleanup, washed my hands, and hustled back to the living room to find Kyle exactly where I'd left him.

"You okay?" I knelt down in front of him on the blanket and was about to ask him if he had changed his mind. The answer came in his actions rather than words. He tumbled me off my knees with a full body check, taking me by such surprise. I yelped and giggled, feeling more buoyant than I could remember feeling in a very long time. The intensity of his amber eyes looking down at me made me sober finally, and I reached up to stroke my hand along his jaw.

"I like you," I said to him quietly.

"I really like you too."

He was nestled between my thighs, so with very little maneuvering, he found his way into my heat with the head of his cock. I opened my legs wider and pulled back at my hips, and with a bit of forward moving pressure, he slid into my body, filling me with his hard shaft. My eyes rolled back as my breath hitched. I still wasn't used to his size, and the initial pain that came with his intrusion sent shivers through my entire body.

"There is nothing better than that first stroke, I swear," I confessed, eyes closed, voice hoarse from pleasure.

Kyle withdrew completely, and my eyes shuttered open to find him with the usual sexy grin, waiting for the visual contact, to reenact the entry. Another full stroke in. Then all the way out. All the way in. All the way out. The intense eye contact and the full length of his impossibly hard shaft lit up my channel with friction as he moved in and out. The pace, excruciatingly slow, created a painful awareness of every single disturbance of matter, air, and even time as it ticked by.

Was there a way to capture it all? To somehow hold every bit of the experience in a snow globe or a diorama or some sort of kaleidoscope? That way I could bring it out when I was lonely and have a look and relive this. Take a trip down memory lane and feel the feelings, smell the smells, taste the tastes. I would be back in the moment. How could I do that? How could I freeze a moment in time?

A tear slid down my temple and got lost in my hairline. I felt his hand before I realized what had happened. Kyle tried to capture it, but it was gone as quickly as it was shed. Unfortunately, tiny friends were right behind in its wake.

"What's this?" he asked in a whisper. "Am I hurting you?"

He sifted his fingertips through my hair while he spoke.

"No." I gave him a wobbly smile. "No. Please. Don't stop. Never mind that." I shook my head lightly away from his caress. "Just hormones." I added an eye roll to punctuate my thoughts on Mother Nature currently. "Please. I'm begging you not to stop. Fuck me. It all feels so good right now," I told him. I rotated my hips the best I could with his weight on top of me. "I want to feel you come more than anything else. Watch your face when you come apart. Fill me, Kyle."

"Skye." He kissed away a tear. "Beautiful girl."

He started thrusting his hips faster, although the pace was still very lazy compared to what I'd seen from him in the past. He kissed my tear-moistened cheeks, following a path to my lips.

I wanted the conversation to cease and the action to pick up. We could dissect my emotional basket-case-ness afterward. The flexing of muscle beneath my fingers encouraged more exploration along his spine and down into the low valley of his lower back. I sank my fingers into the thick mounds of flesh of his ass and groaned with him.

"You are amazing, Kyle," I said. "So good, you feel so good, inside and out. I just can't get enough. I feel like I can't get you deep enough inside me." I pulled him closer and closer to my body every time he thrust forward, lifting my legs to wrap around his waist.

"Aahhh, that's it. Can you feel me deeper now?" he asked between lunges.

"I can," I gasped. "You're right, it's so good."

"Hook your arms under your knees," he told me, still

seated deep inside. "Good, Rocket, yeah, up by your elbow. Pull back really far, lift your ass and pussy up high in the air."

I must have looked like I was stuck in the midst of doing a backward roll. My chin was tucked to my chest and my legs were nearly flipped back over my head, offering my opening straight up toward the ceiling. Kyle stood up and then squatted to line himself up, just before driving straight down into my sex.

"Holy—" Sound was cut off from my throat from the intense impact crashing through my body.

He drove into me again and again in that position, literally drilling down into my pussy with his cock until I saw stars. Oxygen was in short supply due to my position and the pace with which he was pounding into me.

"Fuck, fuck! Skye! I'm going to come, baby. I'm going to fill your cunt so deep, you're going to feel me in your throat, Rocket."

"Yes! God, yes, do it. Come, Kyle. Please!"

Kyle fucked me a few more times and then froze, sucking in a deep breath through his nose. He was so beautiful to watch as he climaxed inside my body, shuddering in a wave from his neck down through his torso, hips, and then all the way down to his feet, where he wiggled and stretched his toes like a cat that had just woken from a long nap in the sun.

He gently pulled out of my body and eased my ass down to the blanket. He collapsed onto the floor beside me, and I rolled over, grabbed the far end of the blanket, and rolled back toward him, covering us as I did so.

We lay in each other's arms for a long time, saying nothing

at all. It was one of the best moments I'd had in a very long time. Certainly, one of the best moments I'd ever shared with a man after sex. Sometimes saying nothing was exactly what the moment called for. Silence had a way of saying so much more than words.

Morning light woke us, and I shot straight up into a sitting position.

"Oh no. Oh shit." I looked around frantically for my phone. I couldn't even remember where I'd set it when we came in the night before. I squinted to see the teeny tiny clock on the stove way across the room in the adjoined kitchen.

"Settle down, woman. It's only six," Kyle mumbled from beside me. "Do you wake up like that every morning? You're going to have a heart attack by the time you're forty." He pulled me back down to lie against him. I resisted at first but quickly gave in to the allure of the warm spot beneath the plaid blanket.

Now that it was light in the room, I could really appreciate the beauty of the pattern and rich blue colors of the cover. I couldn't help but wonder if it was an heirloom too. It was so hard to find craftsmanship like that in modern-day stores.

When I moved again, I realized the even bigger mistake I'd made than not setting an alarm. "Oh God. Oh shit."

"What now?" he mumbled again, rolling onto his back, clearly giving up any hope of a few more minutes of sleep.

"I never got back up after we—"

"Can't follow. Need coffee."

"I'll take this blanket with me when I go. If it's ruined, I'll replace it. Although, if we're being honest with ourselves, it's really your fault," I said, looking around, trying to figure out a plan to get from the living room to the bathroom without looking like a stabbing victim.

"Oh, my God, will you stop? Who cares about the blanket? Is there even an issue?" He finally caught on to why I was freaking out. Thank God he had hardwood floors and not carpet.

I knew what had happened without looking. I could feel it when I moved. "Oh yeah, there's an issue, all right. Do you mind if I hop in the shower before I head home?"

"Not at all. I'll go set some towels out."

While he did that, I quickly folded the blanket with all the evidence doubled to the inside so it couldn't be seen and set it on the floor by the front door. I took my clothes out but left my bag and purse on top of the blanket so I could scoop it all up on my way out.

After a quick shower, I nearly plowed my sexy man over as I hurried out of the bathroom.

"Where's the fire? I was just bringing you a cup of coffee." He offered me one of the ceramic cups in his hand, and I couldn't help but smile at the sweet gesture.

"Thank you. It smells heavenly." I inhaled the aroma wafting up from the UCLA mug. "Nice touch." I grinned, gesturing toward the cup with my chin.

"Why do I have a feeling you can't wait to get out that door, though?" He narrowed his eyes while taking a sip from his own coffee.

"I have a million things on the calendar again today. Don't you?"

"Yeah." He sighed. "I can't bring myself to look at my

email, though, so I spent half the time you were in the shower looking at baby goat videos on Facebook instead."

"You did not," I accused him with a smile before taking another sip from my cup.

"Have you ever watched one of those? Even just one and you're hooked. Twenty minutes later, and you're wondering what happened to all the time you'll never get back." He leaned against the doorjamb of the bathroom while he spoke.

What would it be like to not have to rush off? To spend the weekend in bed together, trading off between laughing and kissing and making love all day? What would a life shared with someone I was actually compatible with be like? My mind raced around to twenty-three different places before—

"Wow. Where are you off to right now?"

"Hmm?" I tried to act innocent while filling my mouth with coffee so I wouldn't have to give an actual answer.

"Well, there's my answer from last night," he said. "You have a terrible poker face, in case no one's ever told you that before." He smirked and ducked when I playfully swung my hand out to smack him.

I swallowed my coffee and answered, "I've gotten into a terrible habit of daydreaming since I've met you. Or, rather, since I've been reacquainted with you."

"Interesting. Dare I ask what the daydream was like?"

"I think I'll keep some things to myself, Mr. Armstrong," I said, the coffee finished. "But I need to go, or I'm going to be sitting in traffic all morning. I need to be at a brunch at a church by ten thirty. Thank you for the coffee, and I guess I'll talk to you later today?"

"I'll walk you out." He followed me toward the front door.

"You don't have to do that. I know you have to get your day started too. Didn't you say you have jury selection today?" I set my mug on the kitchen counter before heading to the front door.

"Yep, but that's not until ten," he said. "Even then, most of the time they start late. Judges love to make everyone wait on them, so they show up late to prove how almighty they are."

"Oh jeez, I thought the mayor was bad with the power flex crap. That would drive me insane. I hate being late, but I hate when others are late even more." I slung my bag and purse over my shoulder and stuffed the folded-up blanket under my arm.

"Let me carry something." He held his arms open to take something, but I stepped into the space instead.

"I like this plan better," I said, looking up at him.

"Me too, actually. Although, I don't like the saying goodbye part. Wish you could stay all day."

"Mmmm, that would be nice," I agreed. "Maybe we could spend a weekend together after the election is over and we can be seen in public."

Kyle kissed me until I was dazed and barely able to stand up straight, and then he moved away to open the front door. He held my gaze while he swung the door open and stepped out into the morning sunshine. It was a perfect autumn sun-up in Southern California. Crisp and fresh, the hint of the smell of a wood-burning fireplace still lingering in the air from the night before.

"Assistant DA Armstrong! Ms. Delaney! So, it's true! Are you two dating? Can we get a quote? A picture?"

A man in plain street clothes stood about ten feet down on the city-owned section of the sidewalk in front of Kyle's house. Another man with an elaborate camera stood beside him, snapping away while we gaped. We'd both looked directly at him, frozen with shock, when he'd said our names. Without thinking, I turned into Kyle's bare torso to shield myself from being photographed, only to create an even more intimate pose for the photographer.

"Get the fuck off my property, or I'll call the police and have you arrested," Kyle warned.

"I'm not actually on your property, Mr. Armstrong, as you can plainly see." The man swept his hand in a wide gesture in front of himself. "But can you tell us how long you and Ms. Delaney have been dating? Does the election make things awkward in the bedroom?"

"Oh, my God." I turned and went back inside Kyle's house. I couldn't very well get in my car and have them follow me to my condo. I had no idea what to do, so I flopped down on his sofa and covered my face with my hands.

Kyle came back inside after a minute or two and approached me like a spooked cat. "I'm sure this isn't as bad as you're painting it out to be in your head right now," he said calmly.

Raising my head, I glared at him before speaking. "Did you recognize that little bastard? He was the one asking us if we matched our outfits the other night! I knew he was acting odd. I fucking knew it. I should've listened to my gut! Goddamn it, Kyle!"

"How can this even be news, Skye? It's a fucking city

council seat. It's not the damn Governor's race. Shit, it's not even the mayor, for Christ's sake." He rubbed the back of his neck as he paced around the room.

"Any chance I had of winning—hell, of just being taken seriously—just went out the front door right beside me." I pointed at the very front door I referred to. "Bailey warned me. She told me to be careful. I have no one to blame here but myself. I tried to be smart about all this, but I failed. I failed at the one thing I wanted more than anything else." I scoffed at how easily my dreams were slipping through my fingers.

Kyle came and knelt on the floor in front of me. His bare torso was a reminder of how fucked up my priorities had become.

"Can you please put some clothes on?" I grimaced while I asked.

"Now I'm offending you? In my own home? You're really something, you know that?" He stood and crossed the room toward the kitchen. Whatever sweet moment he was going to attempt, I'd just blown to smithereens. He grabbed a T-shirt from a small pile of folded laundry and roughly pulled it over his head.

"Well, I've been called worse," I said. "And I'm sure the press is about to give it their best shot too."

"Is that all you ever worry about? I mean, when all is said and done, what the press thinks? What does the public think about you? What hit your career will take?" His voice grew louder and louder with each question.

"It's easy for you to stand there and judge me." I stood to square off with him.

"And that means what, exactly?" He looked at me with a mixture of frustration and challenge.

"I didn't start my life with privileges more plentiful than I could catalog, Kyle, based on my gender." I could hear the bitter edge in my voice because I tended to take enormous pride in my accomplishments, especially because of where I'd had to start.

"But you think I did?" He screwed his face up with the offense.

I shrugged. "If the shoes fit, right?"

Folding his arms across his chest in defiance, he said, "You're so out of line right now. But please"—he waved me on—"continue. I'd love to know where this is going. I assume you actually have a point other than insulting me for once?"

I narrowed my eyes at his dig. "The point, Counselor, is that I've had to bust my ass to get where I am. I've spent years as a lowly staffer for pork-bellied elected boneheads."

I looked through the blinds to see if the reporter was still out front and was relieved to see he and the photographer had left, apparently satisfied with the information they'd gotten.

"I've been proving my worth in this fucking town since the day I picked this career path. *That*, Mr. Armstrong, is the part you really will never understand. Because *that*, whether you want to believe it or not, is the ugly truth." I walked toward the front door and picked up my stuff from where I had dropped the heap when I came back in. Turning back to Kyle, I finished my diatribe. "A woman is not treated equally, especially in a 'good old boys' industry like this one. So by doing the walk of shame for the photographer camped in front of your house this morning?" With my hand on the doorknob, I looked at him and shrugged. "I just undid all the years of hard work I had done up to now."

I let myself out and closed the door quietly as I left. I prayed he wouldn't make another scene and follow me out front. Stuffing my bag and his blanket in my trunk, I listened for Kyle's front door to open, but he never came after me. He allowed me the shred of dignity I clung to, and I drove home in silence. I considered calling Bailey to tell her what had happened but couldn't bring myself to do it just yet. Laura was another temptation, but I didn't want to keep stressing her out. And Oliver would just tell me to go back and apologize and stop being so dramatic about everything.

Even though I'd taken a shower at Kyle's, I took another one when I got home. I stood under the hot spray and let the water clear my thoughts. Eventually, when the water ran cold, I knew I had to face the world. I really needed to get my head back in the game and put the "waaaambulance" in park once and for all.

Mistakes were made. No doubt about it. However, I had a full schedule to contend with and votes to secure. None of which would happen while I sat around feeling sorry for myself.

An extra strong cup of coffee and a big bowl of Cocoa Puffs later, and I was geared up to call Bailey. My phone rang just as I unlocked the screen to dial, startling me so I lost my grip and juggled the device like I was playing a solo round of Hot Potato.

"Shit! Shit!" I said, trying to catch the thing before it hit the granite countertop or tile floor.

"Hello?" I answered blindly, happy to not have cracked the screen on a hard surface.

"Good morning, Skye. Hope I didn't catch you at a bad time?" Bailey's voice filled the line.

"Hey there." I breathed a sigh of relief that it wasn't *him*. "Nope, I was just unlocking my screen to call you, actually." I slumped down onto the stool at the breakfast bar.

"About the posts on Instagram, Facebook, and Twitter, I'm guessing?" she asked, cutting right to the chase.

"Ummm, I haven't looked at socials yet this morning, but I can explain." I should've known she'd drop the hammer right out of the gate, yet somehow I still wasn't prepared.

"What's to explain?" she asked blandly. "It's pretty self-explanatory."

"I know what it looks like, but I want you to know that I haven't been ignoring the advice you've given me, Bailey. I truly value your opinion and the experience you bring to the table. I mean, I was being—"

"Skye?" Bailey cut me off before I could fall on the proverbial sword.

"Hmmm?"

"I think we're talking about two different things. Kyle Armstrong withdrew from the city council race about thirty minutes ago. His camp announced it on all their social media channels as well as their official website. He's out." Bailey's tone was still very matter-of-fact. Even significant news like that didn't elicit emotion.

Words escaped me. Oxygen sort of did too.

"You still there?" she finally asked.

"Yeah. I'm here," I croaked.

"Okay, I can hear by your tone this is news to you, too. I was under the impression you were with him last night by the picture I saw on the *Daily Talk's* Twitter post. Where am I getting my wires crossed?"

"You're not" was all I could really offer in the way of response. I wasn't sure if I was happy or mad. Did I want to call him or completely ignore him?

Regardless, I had a brunch to be at in less than an hour, and if I didn't get my ass in gear, I'd be late or a no-show completely.

"I need to go, Bailey. I have to be at that church thing in less than an hour. Whatever it is, I can't even think straight right now. Oh, man. I really didn't see this coming. Well, maybe a little. He said something last night, but I thought he was just venting, I guess."

"Okay, go! Get ready, get your shit together, and drive safely. We can talk later about all of this. I'll do damage control about the picture, but really, with him out of the race, it doesn't even matter. He did you a huge favor there." She ended her sentence with a halfhearted chuckle.

Of all the damn times for her to finally show emotion.

Boy, did those words sting. Even though she didn't mean them to, they struck me in the heart like an arrow. Had Kyle given up on the election for me? Did he withdraw because of the whining I did in his living room before I left that morning? Did he actually yield his desires to mine? I would never forgive myself if that were the case.

Unfortunately, we'd have to explore all of that later. I had to put on my charming face and get out and meet some voters.

CHAPTER TEN

I was becoming a master at faking my way through events while my heart was breaking into a million pieces inside my chest. If I thought too long about it, I would be concerned about what that said about my psychological well-being in general. But on the surface, I told myself I was doing what needed to be done to get through the election. One event at a time, one day at a time. Usually it was more like one hour at a time and, in some cases, one minute at a time.

The largely female brunch crowd was both receptive and supportive. The women asked great questions, and I was able to add several new topics to my organic platform—as Bailey and I had taken to calling it. I tried to adapt the topics I spoke about, depending on the crowd in attendance, in an effort to keep the audience engaged and participatory. By the end of the brunch, I felt more like I had gained a room full of new aunts and grandmas rather than voting hopefuls. I couldn't really ask for more than that.

Once I was back in the confines of my car, I powered on my phone, and it blew up with notifications. Text messages from Oliver and Laura outnumbered all the others, but the one that grabbed my immediate attention wasn't from them.

You're supposed to pick up when I call.

A smile overtook my entire face. He certainly knew how to grab my attention. Unfortunately, the call he referred to had come just as I went into the brunch and turned my phone off. His text was received only minutes after the unanswered call. By that point, hours had passed and I hadn't responded.

Now what? How to play the response? It was the only message he'd sent. Nothing more after that one call and text. I quickly looked at the other calls, many from news outlets wanting interviews or quotes about Kyle dropping out of the race. Some just wanted a sit-down with a candidate in general. Pretty typical stuff from what I'd experienced while working with Hardin.

I forwarded those to Bailey to schedule interviews or send press kits. Often that would be enough information for the reporter to write his piece and an actual personal interview wouldn't be necessary.

One of the notifications on my phone was a cancellation of my midafternoon event, creating an unexpected block of free time. I didn't have to be anywhere until a Chamber of Commerce mixer, as it was called, at six o'clock that evening. I got on the road, still wearing a goofy smile, and headed back to my condo.

I decided to really put my heart on the line and ask Kyle to be my date for the event. It would do double duty in showing him I really wanted to be serious about things between us and a sort of coming-out to the public and press that we were dating. Fear niggled at me terribly, though, that he would turn me down after the horrible way we'd parted this morning.

I took the total coward's approach and sent him the

invitation via text message at the next red light.

> *Would you please be my date at the*
> *Chamber Mixer tonight at six?*

I hit Send and held my breath. It reminded me of the first night I'd invited him to my house for the booty call that started this entire wild ride. Who knew I'd be sitting in this position, ready to tell the man I had genuine feelings for him.

Jesus Christ. I was falling for him. Maybe, if I could be one hundred percent honest with myself, I'd admit I'd already fallen.

I am in love with Kyle Armstrong.

I tossed the idea around in my mind like a load of laundry on fluff. Warm and comforting, familiar and safe. Yep, I was in deep shit.

But Rome wasn't built in a day, as the saying goes.

Traffic began to move again, so I couldn't stare at my phone and overanalyze what was happening with the message. I set my device in the cup holder and drove the rest of the way home. Once parked in my designated spot, I grabbed all my stuff from the passenger seat, then hummed as I strolled through the condo complex toward my ground-floor unit.

What the hell was I going to wear to this mixer tonight? My closet was getting a serious workout with all the public appearances, and my dry-cleaning bill was bigger than I'd ever seen. My phone's ringing snapped me out of my wardrobe conundrum, and I rummaged through my handbag to find it.

"Hello?" I said hurriedly when I finally got the device to my ear.

"Hey."

The automatic smile was back. It was Kyle.

"Hey yourself," I said through my grin. "Are you busy? Sorry to bother you at work."

"We're on a short recess." He sighed. I could hear the tension in his voice and could picture him rubbing the back of his neck. "It's ridiculous here today. I kind of figured it would be. I wanted to talk to you instead of texting, though. Can you talk?"

"Yeah, your timing is perfect, actually. I just got home. My afternoon event canceled, so I just have that mixer tonight. So, what do you think? Want to go?"

"I would love to." I could already hear the reservation in his answer. "But I don't think I'll be out of here in time to get to that side of town. I'm really sorry."

"Oh, what a bummer." I didn't bother hiding my disappointment.

"I'm sorry, Rocket."

"Don't worry about it. I'll get someone else to go with me. You know these things suck when you're standing around by yourself. It's fine," I said, trying to ease his guilt. Worrying about little nonsense like a Chamber of Commerce mixer was the last thing he needed on his mind.

"No."

"Sorry?"

"No one else."

"Uh. Okay? Not sure what that means, exactly?"

"I don't want you going with another guy. That's what *that* means."

"Boy, I guess I should've pegged you for a caveman." I chuckled so he wouldn't miss the lightheartedness behind the comment.

"The cuneiform was on the wall," he said without skipping a beat.

"Good one, Counselor. Good one!" Had to give him props for the comeback.

"Skye. In all seriousness, we need to talk."

"Ya think?" I shot back dryly.

"I'm sure the news of me dropping out of the election blindsided you this morning, and I want to apologize for that. We didn't really part on warm fuzzies, did we?"

"No, we didn't. And I'm the one who needs to apologize for being such a bitch to you. I could blame the shock of the reporter out front, the panic of speculating about the ramifications. Whatever. It doesn't excuse my behavior because you weren't responsible for any of those things."

"Well, we can take turns doing penance later. How's that?"

"Okay, but you go first." I laughed, trying to make light of the heavy conversation. I really didn't want to screw up this relationship. God, not already.

"Can I come over after the mixer?" he asked. "I don't anticipate being super late here, but I don't think I can be back over to Sun Valley or Shadow Hills by six. Probably not even seven."

"Deal. Why don't you text me when you're leaving the courthouse, and I'll get out of the mixer and meet you at my place?" I suggested.

"All right, that's a good plan. It'll give me something to look forward to. I have some other big news to tell you about too." His voice switched to a completely different type of excitement then.

"Tell me!" I was the worst at having to wait. For anything.

"Nope. You'll have to wait until tonight," he taunted. "It will give you something to look forward to as well."

"Oh, my God." I bounced up and down like a five-year-old. "I love and hate surprises. Now I'll be texting you all day trying to guess."

"Well, my phone goes off once I'm back in the courtroom, so don't be disappointed when I don't respond. Judge's rules. And if a phone notification sounds, even on vibrate, there's serious hell to pay. I've seen this particular judge hold people in contempt for it. I don't fuck with it," he said in complete honesty.

"Oh, wow. Okay, I won't bug you," I promised. "But I'm already counting the minutes until I see you tonight."

Whoa, where is this girlfriend stuff coming from? And why does it feel so good?

"Did you just hear yourself being sweet to me?"

"I know. Scary, right?" I whispered, covering my mouth with the tips of my fingers.

"Just a little. But I could really get used to it." I could almost hear the smile on his face. "I'll talk to you later."

Then he was gone, and I was left holding the phone up to my ear with a smile on my face to match the one I heard on his, listening until the dial tone went to that horrible *bonk bonk bonk* sound.

◆ ◆ ◆ ◆

By the time I heard the knock on my front door, my mind was exploding with a rush of nervous excitement. I still wore the dress I'd worn to the mixer tonight, complete with the lingerie I'd donned knowing Kyle would be coming over.

There was a hungry look in his eyes when I opened the door, and I sucked in a rush of air before he mashed his mouth to mine and kicked the front door closed with his foot as he backed me into the wall of the entryway.

"Well," I gasped. "Hello."

When he finally broke away, his eyes glittered in the dim light of my condo. He pressed his forehead to mine, then rubbed his cheek along the one side of my hairline, inhaling. He continued to nuzzle along toward my ear, where he kissed and licked me, sending a brilliant chill through my entire body.

"I was worried I'd never have the chance to feel you again. To smell you or taste you. I was so worried I'd fucked it all up this morning when you left my place." He pulled back to look at me directly. "I didn't like that feeling at all, Rocket. It was bad. It felt really, really bad."

"I know." I nodded. "I didn't like it either. I don't want to do that again. Usually when I walk away, I don't care. I don't look back. But I can't do that this time. Let's not do that again, okay?"

"Okay." He kissed me again, holding my face still in his hands while he peppered every feature with attention. The hunger and need that normally drove our passion seemed to be ramped even higher.

"Wait." I tried to speak between kisses. "Wait, Kyle. I need to know two things, please. I've been going crazy all day."

He grinned because he already knew what I was going to ask him. He'd dangled a carrot in front of me earlier by saying he had exciting news to share, and I'd been going out of my mind waiting to hear.

"Grab some water bottles while I tell you," he instructed, walking to the front door to make sure we were locked up for the night.

I grabbed a few bottles from the fridge and turned out the light, and we headed to the bedroom.

"Oh, my God, don't make me ask you again. I'm going crazy." I whimpered.

"Okay, okay." We each went to opposite sides of the bed and started taking the pillows off. He spoke while we worked on the covers.

"There were some big things going on at work. I didn't want to mention anything about it for several reasons. Mostly, I'm superstitious as hell, as ridiculous as that sounds, and I didn't want to jinx it. Are you familiar with the structure of the DA's office?" he asked, sitting on the bed.

"Not really, if I'm being honest. I know you guys have at least three floors, so there must be a lot of you."

"That's putting it mildly. It's a big city, for one thing, and it's a big department, for another. So very basically, there's the DA, the Chief Deputy DA under him, and then the department branches out in three directions." He gave me a questioning glance to make sure I was still following.

"Still with you so far. Sort of like subdivisions?" I asked to simplify the whole conversation.

"Kind of. There's line operations, special operations, and administration. Each of those subdivisions is broken down into smaller divisions and on and on. As the grand jury advisor, I worked under the Special Operations Assistant DA."

"Right. I remember you telling me that when you formally introduced yourself to me." I grinned, remembering that day at city hall.

"Well, now I *am* the Special Operations Assistant DA."

Pride beamed from his face after he'd finished his last sentence, and I was so happy for him. I launched myself across the bed and into his arms, hugging him and kissing him in celebration.

"I'm so proud of you! Good job! I didn't know you were up for a promotion, or applying for a new job, or however this all works, but I'm so happy and proud that it happened. I'll learn all the workings of your department, I promise!" I held my hand up like a good Scout would while making a guarantee.

"It's only been a couple of weeks, and we haven't spent much time talking about our day jobs. But that doesn't change the fact that I'm happy for you." I kissed him again and gave him another squeeze. "And so very proud."

Kyle took my hands. His face grew very serious. "Do you understand why I had to drop out of the election, Skye? There were two reasons. There was no way I could continue to effectively campaign and, on the very slim chance I won the city council seat, do justice by the constituents."

He squared his body to mine and really held my hands firmly, seeming to want to make sure he had my full attention when he spoke the next part. "More important than any of that is you. Do you understand that?"

I stared at him for a moment, prompting him to repeat himself.

"Do you understand what you've come to mean to me in such a short amount of time?" He tugged on my hands, signaling my moment to answer.

"It's really beginning to dawn on me," I said, realizing he needed a verbal response.

"I don't know how this all happened. I came up to you at Itza's that night, thinking maybe we could hook up at best," he said and laughed quietly, as if laughing at himself. "Never in a million years did I think our connection would be as off the charts as it is. At least for me. I can only speak for myself here. But I was not about to watch you walk out of my life this morning and that be the end of it. I couldn't give up on something that has this kind of potential. Not for something that was more of a whim than anything else."

"Wow." I took a deep breath and let it out, causing Kyle to grin. He was already becoming familiar with my quirky habits, like how I started deep conversations. "I feel like a thank you is in order for all of that." I motioned toward the space in front of him, as if all the words he just spoke were on a big pile on the bed between us. "You're so brave. I hope I can learn some of that from you. You're very good at expressing your feelings. I'm just a beginner, so bear with me."

Another big breath in, then out, in an attempt to fortify my courage. "I was so worried that you had thrown in the towel because of the whining fit I threw this morning. I knew better, logically. Your conviction is much stronger than that—to be diverted by a pissy girl. But I was afraid our hearts were leading us to do things that weren't true to our minds. I want us both to promise we will never try to manipulate the other or try to derail the other's career for selfish reasons. We've both worked too hard in our chosen careers to behave like that. And if we both care for each other, as I think I'm hearing us say we do, that's definitely not the way you treat someone you love."

The moment the words came out of my mouth, I realized the slip up, and my hand flew to my lips. There was no way to recall them at that point, however. My eyes widened to their limits while I watched Kyle like a hawk. The next move was his and his alone.

"Were you drinking tonight?" he asked plainly.

"No. Just iced tea. The usual when I'm driving."

I was like a statue as he stood from where he was sitting on the bed and started unknotting his tie. He left the ends to hang on either side of his neck while unbuttoning his cuffs. Next, he worked all the buttons down the placket of the shirt and pulled the tails from his slacks, keeping his steady gaze on me the entire time.

"So, Rocket, how do you propose we spend the first night of what I hope is the rest of our lives together, hmmm?"

"I think I can come up with a few ideas." I looked up at him with a mischievous grin. Life would never be dull with this man. That was for certain.

EPILOGUE

"Let's just run through it one time. For practice." I followed Kyle through the bedroom of his bungalow, toweling off my freshly showered hair. I had pulled on some panties and one of his T-shirts to sleep in before I came out of the bathroom.

"You're going to be great. You're stressing over nothing—gee, imagine that?" he responded casually.

I playfully smacked his chest as he walked by where I sat on the end of the bed to brush through my hair. It was very distracting when Kyle paraded around without a shirt, sinful pajama pants hanging loose and low on his toned hips. My eyes roamed all over his muscular body, and I subconsciously licked my lips.

"See something that interests you?" he teased, yellow cat eyes glowing with delight.

"Indeed, I do, Counselor. But stop trying to distract me! Won't you help me practice my speech?" I gave him the best puppy-dog eyes I could manage. "Please? Just one run-through? I have my notes right here." I knelt up on the mattress excitedly as he sauntered closer, looking like I'd finally reeled him in.

He held out his hand for what I thought was the note

cards, but instead of taking them from me to use as a guide, he tossed the small white notes over his shoulder and circled my wrist with his fingers instead.

"Stand up, Rocket. Feet on the floor."

I moved without thinking twice, bringing my body flush against his, my nose seeking the delicious hollow just below his Adam's apple. He always smelled so good in that little dip, and I couldn't resist nibbling the taut skin there while inhaling his sexy scent.

"Stop."

A whimper escaped through my parted lips, and I slid my gaze up to meet his. "You're right. Sorry. You said you'd help me practice."

"No. You said you wanted me to help you. I think you're overthinking it, so I'm going to distract you instead."

"Wait. I didn't agree to that plan."

"You will," he growled, already kissing the sensitive skin just below my ear while skating his palms across my ass. My handsome man knew every move that lit my nerves ablaze, and he was a dirty player when he wanted to be. Kyle gathered my wet hair into one fist and tugged my head swiftly to the side. The pain zipping across my scalp transformed into erotic pleasure each time he increased the tension. With his skillful mouth, he made a path up and down my neck, nipping and kissing the delicate skin with just enough aggression to make my core pulse with need.

"Kyyylle," I drew out his name in protest, but it was useless. Already tugging my panties to the side, his deft fingers found the needy center of my pussy wet for him. The rumble that worked up from low in his chest vibrated through both our bodies.

"Oh baby, feel how wet you are." He swirled his fingers around the outside of my pussy but didn't push inside.

"I know. It would be a terrible tragedy to let all that go to waste." I tried swiveling my hips, chasing his fingers with my movements in order to work him where I needed him most.

He chuckled into the crook of my neck. "Woman, be still." Kyle gripped my waist with his other hand to hold me in place.

"What? It's true!" I said, trying to keep a serious look on my face. "You don't want to be responsible for wasting precious natural resources, do you?"

"What about your speech?" he taunted before treating me to one of his powerful, drugging kisses. The kind that left me breathless and dizzy and wondering how the entire room had turned upside down and no one else seemed to notice but me.

"What speech?" I said hazily as I rocked against his fingers that were buried inside me again. "Jesus Christ," I panted. "Why does every single thing you do feel so good?" I leaned my forehead into his chest to stay upright while he pumped his hand faster. Harder.

"Because I love you. And you can feel the difference."

I snapped my eyes open and stared up to his, but the emotion I expected to wash over me didn't come. Instead of ice-cold dread and panic smacking me in the face and destroying the blissful torrent of endorphins he was encouraging to surge through my system, I was blanketed in radiant warmth, like basking in the summertime sun.

"Kyle?"

"Hmm?" he asked casually, as if he hadn't just declared his love for me. As if he weren't plunging his thick fingers deep inside me while he spoke. This man would always be my steady wall of safety. He would be the calm in my storm, the trusted partner in my adventures, and the very capable, dominant lover in my bed. He was a dream come true, and somehow, I hadn't run him off.

"I love you too." For the first time in my life, I gave those words to a man, and nothing ever felt more right.

In one fluid motion, he scooped me up off my feet and carried me to his bed, laying me down and quickly climbing on above me. Kyle was inside me, thrusting and pumping so quickly, I couldn't imagine when he'd shed his pants. The frenzy built to a climax between us, with both of us whispering how much we loved one another, how we needed one another, and in moments, I was shouting his name with my release. Kyle followed right after, pulling his cock from my body and coming across my stomach and thighs since he hadn't taken the time to put on a condom. I would never grow tired of seeing him mark me that way, regardless. It was so raw and primal, and it turned me on beyond words.

Perfection. He was perfection.

And he was mine.

The next day, Kyle stood off to the side of the stage as I gave my acceptance speech to the crowd of supporters that gathered at city hall. I happily became the city council representative for the seventh district of the City of Los Angeles and swore before my family and friends to uphold the law and city's charter to the best of my ability.

My mother's eyes brimmed with tears, and mine were a matching pair. Rushing into Kyle's arms after the formal ceremony was over—finding my safe, happy place—made everything right again. He was getting along famously with my mom, and my heart was full to the point it felt like it might burst.

All felt right in the world. Bailey and Oliver stood hand in hand, and even Laura had a rosy glow she couldn't hide. I was happier than I could ever remember being because I had the love of the kindest, most generous man I'd ever known.

We were all on track to live happily ever after.

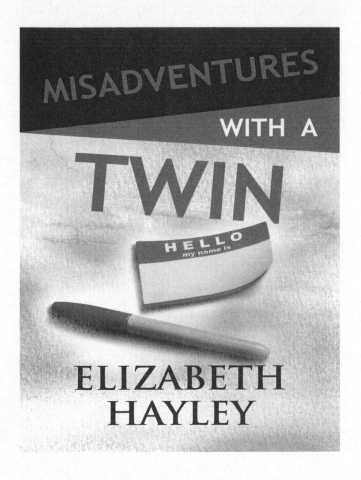

Keep reading for an excerpt!

EXCERPT FROM
MISADVENTURES WITH A TWIN

Looking into those dark-green eyes that stared back into mine, I silently thanked myself for not leaving earlier when I'd spilled red wine on my dress. It wasn't that people could necessarily see it—the dress was dark and so was the room—but I've always been someone who believed in subtle signs. Like an umbrella not opening right when it begins to rain or charcoal toothpaste leaving black marks on my teeth before a date. They were the universe's signals to me that I should stop what I'm doing and turn back or not even leave my house to begin with. That it was time to retreat because the mission was compromised.

Abort, abort, my brain had screamed after my wine spill. Tomorrow was another day, and I could try again. Or not, because my ten-year high school reunion only happened once, and there was no way my friends would have let me ditch them.

Truthfully, this whole reunion thing wasn't exactly my scene, but Becca and Trinity had begged me to go. In high school, it had always been the three of us, and they said the thought of attending an event like this without me would be akin to TLC performing after Left Eye's accident. I'd pointed out that they *did*, in fact, perform again after the singer's death, but my friends weren't having it. I wasn't sure my absence would've had quite the same effect, but nonetheless, I acquiesced. And I was glad I did.

"You remember Mr. Simpkiss, right?"

He thought for a few seconds. "The physics teacher?"

I nodded, smiling. "Did you hear why he left the year after we graduated?"

"No. I didn't know he left at all." CJ seemed interested, his head resting on his palm as he leaned casually on the bar, waiting for me to continue.

"Yup. He got Mindy Tatum pregnant." I expected his eyes to go wide and his jaw to drop, but he looked confused than anything.

"I'm not sure I know a Mindy..."

"You don't remember Mindy? She was in Mr. Simpkiss's class with us senior year." Still nothing. "She had to use that emergency shower thing because her lab partner combined the wrong chemicals or something one day."

"I must've been absent that day," he said, his expression falling like he was sad he'd missed it. I'd have sworn he was there, but it was impossible to be sure about something that happened a decade ago.

"Well, anyway, Mindy posted a picture of her ultrasound during her first semester of college and tagged Mr. Simpkiss in it. Turns out they'd been"—a shiver ran down my body with the thought of the divorced forty-year-old—"dating since right after graduation."

There was the openmouthed stare I'd been hoping for. "No shit. That's crazy. I didn't think Simpkiss had it in him." He paused for a second. "Wait, do you think he was... they were... Did he get fired because something happened *before* Mindy graduated? That's so messed up."

I shrugged. A part of me felt guilty that I was using Mindy's story as entertainment, but CJ seemed interested, so I continued. "The heart wants what the heart wants, I guess."

"I guess."

I laughed, but it was more out of embarrassment than humor. "I'm horrible at small talk."

"Everyone's that way sometimes." Whether it was because of the overhead lights or because I wanted them to, his eyes twinkled when he smiled.

"Not you," I said, my voice more serious than it had been. "You could always talk to anyone. You're naturally friendly."

He was quiet as he ran his fingers over the condensation of his glass. "I try," he said. "But sometimes it's just good acting."

"Are you acting now?"

His mouth parted, but he didn't speak right away. Instead, the left side of his lip quirked up in that way that made me imagine what it would be like to kiss it.

"No," he said softly. "I'm enjoying talking to you."

"Me too."

"Do you want to go somewhere that's a little quieter to

talk?" he asked.

"I actually think I've had enough talking," I said. And then I did something I never would've had the guts to do last time we saw each other.

I leaned in to kiss him. I didn't worry if he'd pull away or if he'd tell me it was nice or that he didn't like me like that or any of the other million reasons I'd used to talk myself out of this in high school. For once, I listened to the beating in my chest that told me just to do it. Make the first move. Be fearless.

His lips touched mine, and I knew it was well worth the risk.

♦ ♦ ♦ ♦

I'd been thinking about this ever since I saw CJ sit down at the bar. The slow but needy grind of our lips against each other's. And as our tongues tangled, I was thankful I'd grown more confident over the years. I didn't even stifle the moan that found its way from my throat to his mouth, and when the vibration of it thrummed between us, he reached a hand around to the back of my neck to deepen our kiss.

My entire body tingled with sensation, like he'd somehow hit every nerve ending with that subtle touch. It had been...well, let's just say it had been a while since a man— especially one as desirable as *this* man—had kissed me like this. Every sweep of his tongue across mine and every soft nip of his teeth on my lip had me forgetting, or simply not caring, that we were behaving like this in public. And if I was being honest with myself, the idea turned me on even more.

But there were things I wanted him to do to me—and things I wanted to do to him—that were definitely not appropriate for public display. The thoughts had me pulling away, breathless. "Would you like to come up to my room? Sorry, is that too forward? Or..." *God, I sound like a hussy.* "I swear I don't make out with men at bars like this all the time. Or ever," I corrected. "But I've had a crush on you since high school, and—"

"So you said." He smiled wide, as if hearing the comment a second time excited him as much as the kiss. And based on the frustrated groan he'd released when I'd pulled away, I'd have guessed he was pretty excited. "Just for the record, I'm not complaining," he added before closing the small distance between our lips again so he could part them with his tongue. He tasted sweet, like rum and mint and something spicy I couldn't identify. "We don't have to go upstairs if you're uncomfortable with it," he whispered against my lips.

"I want to" was the only reply I could find. My attraction to him was even stronger tonight than the girlish crush I'd had on him years ago. Maybe it was something about seeing him all grown up. The long stubble on his jawline that looked like it might grow into a full beard before the night was over. It had me wondering what it might feel like between my legs. *God help me.* Or it might have been his casual confidence and how easily we'd talked. Whatever it was about this man, I wanted him.

"Just know you have my word that I'm not going to tell the guys in the locker room after practice about whatever happens between us. This isn't high school, Zara. We're two consenting adults. Two consenting, very turned-on adults. Speaking for myself at least." He cleared his throat and shifted on the bar stool, drawing my attention to the bulge in his perfectly fitted dark jeans.

"That applies to me too," I said, feeling the blush spread across my cheeks. What had gotten into me? "So before I go back to the old Zara and let my inhibitions dictate my actions, I'd like to formally invite you back to my hotel room, Mr. Jensen."

His smile broadened into a ridiculous grin. "In that case, I'd like to accept, Ms. Pierce."

And with that, I grabbed my bag, downed the last of my Cabernet, and headed toward the elevators.

Once inside, our hands were everywhere. Mine slipping down his back to squeeze his muscular ass. His sliding up the outside of my thigh. And as his cock rubbed against my lower stomach, I wondered if we'd even make it to my room before I had him undressed. His chest was firm against mine. I wanted to feel every part of him at once—his lips on my nipples and between my thighs, his cock spreading me wide.

"God, you're sexy," he said against my collarbone. "Makes me so hard."

I wanted to tell him that he was sexy too. That I was so fucking wet already, he could use my thong as a Slip ' N Slide if he wanted to. But all that came out of my mouth was something completely unintelligible that manifested itself as an unsteady moan.

We broke contact just long enough to exit the elevator and make our way down the short hallway. I fumbled with the key card, playfully swatting his hand away from its place on my hip as he stood behind me, his rock-hard cock pressing against my ass. "If you keep that up, I'll never get this thing open."

He laughed softly, reaching around to place his hand on mine to steady it enough to key us in. Once we were both inside, he spun me against the door, pinning my hands over my head with one of his. I loved when guys took control like this, letting me feel instead of think. And all I wanted to do was feel. Feel his fingers and tongue inside me, feel how thick and hard his cock was in my hand before I felt it fill me.

"What do you want?" he asked. He waited for the answer like it would not only turn him on, but also so he could ensure he wasn't doing more than I was comfortable with.

"Your mouth," I whispered.

He released my hands. "Like this?" he asked, and I gripped his hair in pleasure as he made his way to the exposed part of my chest right above my dress.

"Lower."

He reached around to undo the clasp at the top and dragged the zipper down slowly. But he didn't let it drop. Pulling the fabric over my shoulder enough to gain access to my breasts, he brought his mouth to them, giving each of them his undivided attention. "How about now?" he asked, working his tongue over my nipple softly before giving it a tug with his teeth.

"Getting warmer," I said.

"I was hoping for hot," he teased.

"Oh, this is definitely hot."

This story continues in *Misadventures with a Twin*!

ACKNOWLEDGMENTS

As always, thank you to the amazing, supportive, and giving-beyond-measure team at Waterhouse Press. The Misadventures Series has been such a fun outlet for me to stretch my creative wings outside the intense process of the more extended series we endeavor to create, and I'm so grateful for the opportunity to be a part of this family.

Thank you to the Maniacs sprinting team, Angel and Meredith, for keeping me on track when my wandering mind has trouble staying on task.

Thank you, Martha Frantz, for keeping VBS a fun, current, and happy place for all our sisters. My heart is so full and content, and the book world is largely responsible.

XOXO VB

MORE MISADVENTURES

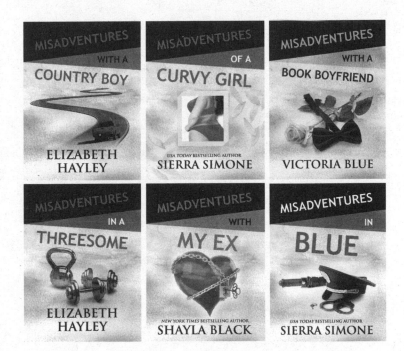

MORE MISADVENTURES

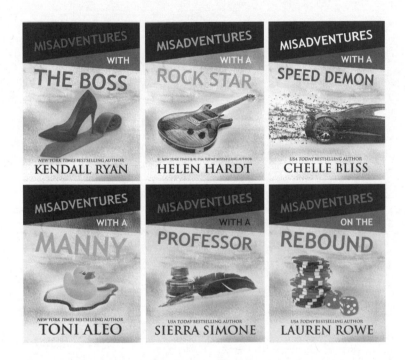